"We swept closer to the other car, moment by moment.

One of the boys twisted backwards in his seat and waved mockingly. Then the Volkswagen sprang ahead with a fresh burst of speed.

"Man!" Eric said, thumping the steering wheel. "What jerks! Man!"

Who's calling who a jerk? I wanted to exclaim. Was this really Eric Moore, always so cool and confident? Eric the star, whom I'd admired since last fall?

"Forget it," I said. "What do you care how fast they go?"

"They're always trying to pull something," Eric fumed. "You don't know—I'll never hear the end of it!"

"Eric!" I cried as he swerved past a line of parked cars. "Slow down, will you!"

"Don't worry," he said. "I'll get us there, okay?"

"Be careful!" I pleaded. "This road has a lot of tricky curves!"

After that, everything is a blur. A screech of brakes. A shout, a slide, a lurch. And after that, I don't remember anything at all. . . .

Why Me?

DON'T CRY FOR YESTERDAY

Why Me?: The Courage to Live
Why Me?: Living With a Secret
Why Me?: No Time to Die

Available from Archway Paperbacks

Why Me?

DON'T CRY FOR YESTERDAY

DEBORAH KENT

SIMON PULSE

New York London Toronto Sydney Singapore

13294228

This book is a work of fiction. Any references to historical
events, real people, or real locales are used fictitiously. Other
names, characters, places, and incidents are the product of the
author's imagination and any resemblance to actual events or
locales or persons, living or dead, is entirely coincidental.

First Simon Pulse edition January 2002

Text copyright © 2002 by Deborah Kent

SIMON PULSE
An imprint of Simon & Schuster
Children's Publishing Division
1230 Avenue of the Americas
New York, NY 10020

Designed by O'Lanso Gabbidon
The text of this book was set in Goudy

Printed in the United States of America
2 4 6 8 10 9 7 5 3 1

Library of Congress Cataloging-in-Publication Data
is available from the Library of Contress.

ISBN 0-7434-0033-X

To Gaylene and Sue,
Adrienne, Patti, and Anne—
All friends for a lifetime.

ACKNOWLEDGMENTS

I would like to thank Susan Nusbaum, Transition Co-ordinator at Access Living of Metropolitan Chicago, for reviewing and discussing this manuscript. I deeply appreciate her thoughtful suggestions.

Why Me?

DON'T CRY FOR YESTERDAY

I

"Okay, let's go over it once more," Katrina said. "Step by step. Take it from the top."

I glanced around uneasily. Anybody could overhear us out here in the crowded hall before the 8:10 bell. "Step One," I began. "We walk down to the Learning Center."

She waited expectantly. "Go on," she said.

"Step Two," I said haltingly. "You'll go in and see where he's sitting. You pull up a chair at his table."

"And?" Katrina prompted.

"And—" This wasn't going to work. Katrina didn't know what she was asking of me.

"You walk up and join us," she filled in. "'Oh, hi, Katrina. Hi Eric.' And you sit down, too. Then, after a minute, I remember something all of a sudden and have to leave—and there you are!"

"And I just ask him to go with me to Cori's party? Just like that? I'll feel like the biggest loser!"

"You?" Katrina exclaimed. "The only reason he hasn't asked you out himself is he's afraid to. He thinks you're so popular you'd never be interested in him."

It was nice to hear her say so. Unfortunately, I didn't believe her. I had plenty of friends, but Eric Moore was out of my league.

Katrina hoisted the bulging green backpack that was her trademark. "You ready?" she asked. "Let's go, before he takes off for homeroom."

"Ready as I'll ever be." I stretched on tiptoe to stash my books on the top shelf of my locker. My blouse crept up my midriff when I reached above my head. Katrina giggled as I tugged it down and tried to tuck it back into place. The dress code at our school was totally repressive, and I was pushing the limits.

Together Katrina and I headed down the hall toward Stairway D. I tried to clear my mind, to sweep away the clutter of worries. I'd been watching Eric since last fall, when he turned up in my American history class. We talked back and forth across the aisle every day. We'd even worked on a group project on the Reconstruction era. But I'd never come anywhere close to a date with him. Asking him to Cori's party would be an all-time first.

Suddenly Katrina put a warning hand on my shoulder. "Uh-oh," she hissed. "Here comes Heartless!"

Sure enough, Mr. Hartman, the school principal, emerged from the stairwell and marched straight toward us. I gave my blouse a desperate yank, but it was too late. I had been spotted.

"You!" Mr. Hartman bellowed. "Come over here!"

All up and down the hall, startled heads turned. Dozens of eyes followed me as I advanced toward my doom, step by heavy step. Katrina tried to follow me, but Mr. Hartman waved her back. "You're fine," he told her gruffly. "But *you!*" he went on, glaring at me, "You're a disgrace! This is a high school, not a dance club!"

I gazed at the floor. If I didn't argue, maybe he'd let me go. We'd still have time to get to the Learning Center if we ran.

"What's your name?" Mr. Hartman demanded.

"Amber Novak."

"Let me see you tuck your shirt in properly, Amber Novak. Go on—tuck it in, right now."

"I can't," I said sadly, with another futile tug. "It's not long enough."

"It's not long enough," he repeated in disgust. "You mean you came to school knowingly wearing a shirt that was too short? That leaves your body exposed?"

Exposed. He made the word sound so ugly, indecent. I wanted to melt into the linoleum.

"You can't go to class like that," Mr. Hartman declared. "Go down to the Main Office."

"Okay," I said meekly. "I'm sorry."

"Next time you'll be sent home," he went on, as if he hadn't heard me. "Today I'll give you a break. See Mrs. Gambino. She'll fix you up."

"Okay," I said again. "Thank you."

"What did you thank him for?" Katrina demanded as we started downstairs. "He just ruined the whole plan!"

"Tell me about it," I muttered. "This is the worst! The worst ever!"

"I'll go to the office with you if you want," Katrina said. "Moral support."

"You sure you want to be seen with me?" I giggled. "This isn't a dance club, you know!"

The moment I set foot in the office, Mrs.

Gambino bustled over to greet me. She was Mr. Hartman's secretary—a nervous little woman with frosted hair who spent most of her time fussing over attendance sheets. "You're Amber Novak," she said, taking me in at a glance. "Come in back, dear. I've got something for you to put on." She made it sound as though I had just stepped out of the shower.

"How did she know I was coming?" I whispered as Katrina and I trailed after her through the maze of offices.

"Cell phone?" she whispered back. "Walkie-talkie?"

"Telepathy?" I suggested. "Maybe he just beams his thoughts to her."

At last Mrs. Gambino led us to a windowless cubicle in the heart of the labyrinth. Next to the computer on the desk stood an old-fashioned electric typewriter, and there was a rickety cabinet in one corner. My stomach knotted with dread as she pulled open one of the lower drawers. "Here you are, dear," she said. "Put this sweater on."

I suppose the object she held out was indeed a sweater by some people's standards—my grandmother's, for instance. Grandma Novak would have thought it was right in style. It was a sickly shade of purple, with big barrel-shaped wooden buttons down the front, and it was enormous. Stretched between Mrs. Gambino's hands it looked like a vast purple tent.

Gingerly I extended my hand to touch the loathsome thing. I had to shut my eyes as I draped it over my shoulders and pushed my arms into the yawning sleeves. The sweater flopped halfway to my knees. I was drowning in its fuzzy purple depths.

Katrina looked on, speechless with sympathy. "Wear it till the end of the day," Mrs. Gambino instructed me. "And don't forget to bring it back at three o'clock."

Forget? I wanted to scream. How could I forget to return it? Did she think I wanted to keep it one nanosecond longer than I had to?

"Thank you," I said, polite to the bitter end. I hesitated. I wanted to ask if I could spend the day in this cubicle. Maybe I could make myself useful, do some typing on that antique machine. I'd do anything to be spared from stepping out into the hall again.

Muffled and distant, the bell rang. "Hurry up and get to your homerooms," Mrs. Gambino said. "You don't want to be marked late!"

Together Katrina and I retraced our steps out to the Main Office. I paused at the door, people streaming past me in the cooridor. There was no escape. I took a deep breath and stepped into the throng. "Now you *really* won't want to be seen with me," I told Katrina. "Pretend you don't know me. I'll understand."

"Tell them it's a new fashion," Katrina said, trying to laugh. "You're out there on the cutting edge."

"Maybe I can die before History," I said hopefully. "That'd be better than having Eric see me like this."

Katrina was determined to come up with solutions. "Hey, you could hunch down and hide your face in it," she suggested. "Maybe no one will recognize you."

"Nice try," I sighed. "Just admit it—this is awful! This is the most awful thing that's ever happened to me!"

"Okay," Katrina said. "I'll admit it's bad. It is definitely the worst kind of bad news."

I was huddled up in my seat in homeroom, trying to ignore the stares and giggles, when Maura Shehan leaned across the aisle and whispered, "They gave you The Sweater, huh?" She said "The Sweater" as if there was only one like it on the planet. She was probably right.

I nodded. "Heartless didn't like my blouse," I

said. "I'd take this thing off, but I'm scared I'll run into him again."

"I had to wear it one day last year," Maura said. "I'll be emotionally scarred for life!"

"That makes two of us," I said. There was comfort in that, knowing I wasn't alone.

As the day passed, I discovered that The Sweater had an impressive history. Everywhere I went, people greeted me and told me their stories. Jeannie Heller had to wear it one day when she was giving an oral presentation in Lit class. Mia Kimball got stuck with it when she had to go up in front of Assembly to receive a Debating Club award. Cara Jablonski told me she'd worn The Sweater on three separate occasions. She even showed me the hole where she got it caught on someone's locker door.

"I'm starting to feel like some kind of folk hero," I told Katrina when I met her in study hall. "The Sweater is like a badge of honor for dress-code criminals!"

"Then you don't need to hunch," Katrina said brightly. "Stand tall and wear it with pride!"

It was wise advice. I couldn't exactly turn The Sweater into a blessing, but it didn't have to be a full-out curse, either. *Stand proud*, I told myself as I set out for History class. *You're wear-*

ing a badge of honor! Display it to the universe!

Room 223 was nearly empty when I arrived. I took my seat at the end of the third row and tried to sit tall as the others straggled in. Heads turned, eyes stared, and mouths dropped open with amazement. "Hey, Granny!" called Mark Spangler. "Bake me some cookies after school?"

I wouldn't let him see me cringe. I'd play right along with him, as if I were wearing The Sweater by choice. "Sure, sonny," I said in a creaky, geriatric voice. "Come on over! I'll even let you borrow my rocking chair!"

I didn't hear Mark's reply. Eric Moore leaned in the doorway. Broad-shouldered and solid, he never quite looked at home in a classroom. The football field was where he shone, where he truly belonged. Now he surveyed the room for a moment as if he were making up his mind whether to go or stay. Our eyes met, and he shook his head in disbelief. I watched breathlessly as he sauntered toward me. "What is that about?" he asked, dropping his backpack with a thump.

"It's about Mr. Hartman doesn't like my fashion statement," I said. "It's about the cabinet in Mrs. Gambino's back cubicle."

Was it only this morning that I'd plotted to

10 *Why Me?*

ask Eric to Cori's party? It was unthinkable now.
He could see through my joking. He knew my
Sweater Pride was just a pretense. Underneath it
all, I was a hopeless loser. Eric could tell. I knew
that he knew.

Eric took his seat across from mine. He
always seemed too big for the desk, his long legs
sprawling into the aisle. "Hey," he said, "you're
in a band, right?"

"How did you hear that?" I asked, aston-
ished. "We're still at the planning stage."

Eric shrugged. "I don't know. Word gets out.
What do you play?"

"I just sing, mostly."

"Oldies?" he asked, eying The Sweater.
"Hey, you could call yourselves Legacy."

"Cool! I like that."

The bell rang. Mr. Spencer marched to the
front of the room and began to scribble on the
blackboard. Then, as the room grew quiet, Eric
bent toward me and whispered, "You want to go
to Cori Madison's party Friday night?"

2

When I look back at that Friday evening, it leaps to my brain in minute detail. I remember getting ready for my date with Eric—taking a long, hot shower, doing my hair, putting on makeup at the bathroom mirror. Twice my little brother Max banged on the bathroom door, yelling for me to hurry up. "I thought maybe you drowned in there!" he grumbled when I finally emerged. "You must've been in the shower forty-five minutes."

"It wasn't all *that* long," I protested. "Come on, I had to wash my hair."

"And dye it, right?" Max asked with all his twelve-year-old sophistication.

"Highlight," I corrected him. "Just to bring out the blonde undertones."

"I'm gonna tell him," Max threatened. "I'll say it'd take an archaeologist to figure out my sister's natural hair color. It's one of the mysteries of the past."

"Ha-ha," I said.

"Are those fake eyelashes?" Max asked. "They're not real, are they?"

I refused to lower myself with a reply. Ignoring him to the hilt, I took a long look at myself in the full-length mirror on my bedroom door. My hair had turned out perfectly. Half a shade lighter than it would be on its own, it puffed softly around my face and fell in smooth ripples below my shoulders. My makeup was flawless. I wore the new tank top I'd bought at the mall just for the occasion. I turned from side to side, checking myself from every angle, imagining how I would look to Eric when he arrived. I'd been dreaming about him for months. Maybe after tonight, he'd start dreaming of me.

I padded downstairs in my stockinged feet, wondering where I'd left my shoes. When I peeked into the den, I found Mom and Dad watching a travel documentary on TV. I even remember what it was about. A team of photographers was climbing into the canopy of the Costa Rican rainforest.

"What's that perfume?" Mom asked, sniffing. "Smells like lilacs."

"It's supposed to," I said. "'An irresistible blend of spring fragrances.'"

"Who is this guy, anyway?" my father inquired. "You haven't even told us his name."

"Eric Moore," I said. "He's on the football team." I hoped that gave him some sort of credentials.

It wasn't good enough. "Where does he live?" Mom asked, and Dad wanted to know, "What do his parents do?"

"Don't ask me!" I said impatiently. "What difference does it make?"

"There are a lot of crazies running around," Dad reminded me. "We just want to make sure he's not an ax- murderer."

"I don't see how you can tell that by where he lives," I said. "You can't predict his sanity by where his parents work, either."

"You're right," Dad sighed. "But still."

I remember my fleeting annoyance at them both. They looked as though they had been middle-aged all their lives. They were so comfortable in the den, with its shelves of books and figurines, and Mom's aquarium bubbling quietly in the corner. They could never understand my excitement about tonight, my eagerness to set off with Eric beside me.

The doorbell rang. Max's feet thudded down the stairs as I dashed into the front hall. My brother was right behind me when I threw the door open. Eric stood on the porch, big and smiling and irresistible. "Hi," he said. "It's hard to find your house, you know that?"

"Yeah," I said. "It's tricky till you know the streets around here." I couldn't wait to get outside. I had to escape before Max said something hideous about my hair or my eyelashes, before Dad popped out to put Eric under interrogation.

"You ready?" Eric asked.

I started to say, sure, I was all set. Then I noticed him staring down at my feet. "Shoes!" I cried, mortified. "Wait till I get my shoes on!"

Max gave a whoop of laughter, and Eric joined in. Hot color surged up my cheeks. So much for my hair, my makeup, my posturing before the mirror. So much for sophistication.

I dashed from room to room and finally found the heels I wanted, right where I'd kicked them off the other day, under the coffee table in the living room. I slipped them on and rushed back to Eric. By now the family had him surrounded. Dad was pumping him about his courses at school, Max was plying him with questions about his red Toyota parked out front, and Mom was warning him to make sure I was home by midnight. If I didn't act fast, we'd never get out alive!

"Come on!" I said. "Let's get going! I promised Cori we'd pick up a pizza on the way."

"You kids have a good time," Mom called as we hurried down the steps. "We'll leave the porch light on for you."

I remember I turned and waved from the front sidewalk. Dad and Max had gone back inside, but Mom watched until we got into the car and fastened our seat belts. Then Eric revved the motor, and we were off.

I looked over at Eric and tried to believe this was real. I, Amber Novak, was on a date with Eric Moore—THE Eric Moore, linebacker for the Eagles. I'd never paid much attention to football until I noticed Eric. Then I started dragging Katrina to all the games just to watch him play, and to wonder if I'd ever get him to notice me. Now we were going to Cori Madison's party. Everyone would see us together.

"You ordered the pizza?" Eric asked, bringing me back to earth.

"Party-size, with everything on it."

"You better tell me where the place is," he said. "I get totally lost around here."

"It's up on Turner Avenue," I said. "You take a right up here at the light."

"Cori throws great parties," Eric said. "I went to one last summer."

"They've got a neat house," I agreed. "There's a pool table in the rec room, and a Ping-Pong table, and all these weight machines."

"You play Ping-Pong?" he asked eagerly.

I shook my head, and Eric frowned. "I shoot pool sometimes," I added, with a hopeful giggle. Eric didn't seem impressed. Apparently Ping-Pong was the game that counted for him.

"Well," he said after a slightly awkward pause, "she'll have good music. I brought a bunch of CDs."

Music was a great conversation topic. He listed the CDs he'd brought, and I told him about the concert I went to last month. By then we had pulled onto Turner Avenue and I directed him to Lil's Pizza, across from the dry cleaner. Parking was tight, as usual. The only place close was in front of a fire hydrant, so Eric waited with the motor running in case he had to move in a hurry. I raced inside, slammed my money on the counter, grabbed the box, and rushed out again. Eric reached across and opened the passenger door for me.

"Come on," he said. "Let's catch those guys up there!"

"What?" I asked, bewildered. The pizza box was so big I had to angle it through the door. I positioned it on my lap, but it was burning hot through the fabric of my jeans.

"Campbell and Marconi and Brooks—you know all those guys, don't you?"

"They're on the team, right?" I tried to steady the box with one hand as I slammed the door with the other. Eric hit the gas and the Toyota leaped forward. The box nearly skidded onto the floor, and I gripped it with both hands. I knew I should refasten my seat belt, but hanging onto the pizza seemed the first order of business.

"Didn't you hear those jerks beeping their horn at me?" Eric asked as we whipped around the corner onto Carpenter Road. "Like, 'Hey man, what're you waiting for?'"

"Is that them?" I asked, catching sight of a green Volkswagen up ahead.

"That's them all right," Eric said. He leaned forward in the driver's seat, as if he could urge the Toyota to go faster by sheer will. We swept closer to the other car, moment by moment. One of the boys twisted backwards in his seat and waved mockingly. Then the Volkswagen sprang ahead with a fresh burst of speed.

"Man!" Eric said, thumping the steering wheel. "What jerks! Man!"

Who's calling who a jerk? I wanted to exclaim. Was this really Eric Moore, always so cool and confident? Eric the star, whom I'd admired since last fall?

"Forget it," I said. "What do you care how fast they go?"

"They're always trying to pull something," Eric fumed. "You don't know—I'll never hear the end of it!"

"Eric!" I cried as he swerved past a line of parked cars. "Slow down, will you!"

"Don't worry," he said. "I'll get us there, okay?"

"Be careful!" I pleaded. "This road has a lot of tricky curves!"

I braced my feet and tried to hold the pizza box level. I remember wondering what the rest of the evening would be like, after such an unpromising start. I imagined sneaking upstairs with Katrina, telling her the whole story, and figuring out some way to go home early. What would Katrina say if I told her Eric Moore was the biggest jerk I'd ever met?

After that, everything is a blur. A screech of brakes. A shout, a slide, a lurch. And after that I don't remember anything at all.

3

━m━

First came the noise. From my floating raft I heard a medley of beeps and rumbles, voices, and a faraway blur of music. I drifted along beneath an arch of overhanging branches that shaded out the sun. The sounds drew nearer—or perhaps I was moving toward them. My raft glided down the stream so slowly, so lazily, it was hard to be sure I was moving at all.

Yet the noise grew louder and more insistent. A voice formed itself into words. "Amber," it said. "Amber, it's time to wake up!"

I opened my eyes, and then shut them hastily against the glaring light. For a few moments more I lay still, waiting for the raft to take me somewhere peaceful again. But the voice wouldn't leave me alone. "Amber," it called. "I know you're awake. Can you hear me?"

Cautiously I stretched my hand over the edge to trail my fingers in the cool water. Instead, I felt the folds of a coarse, dry blanket. Startled, I opened my eyes. A strange face hovered above me, a woman's face with dark curly hair and a hopeful smile.

The smiling lips moved. The stranger was speaking to me. "Don't worry," she murmured. "You're going to be all right."

Why did she think I might worry? I wondered. I was on my way, floating downstream. I'd be perfectly all right if she'd let me go.

But the water had disappeared. Maybe the raft had run aground. It was still now. Motionless. The lights blasted into my face and the woman with the smile insisted, "Can you hear me, Amber? Can you answer me?"

"Hi," I said. "Where am I?" When I spoke, I felt as though the inside of my throat had been scraped raw. I'd never had such a terrible sore throat in all my life.

"You're at Alice Hamilton Hospital," the woman said, and my gaze took in her white nurse's uniform. "You're in the I.C.U."

My brain struggled to make sense of her words. "I see you?" I repeated. For a moment I thought she was inviting me to play some sort of children's game.

"I.C.U. stands for Intensive Care Unit."

"Like in the hospital?" I asked. In the next instant I remembered that was precisely what she had just told me.

"Alice Hamilton," she said again. "In Chicago."

I tried to sit up, to get a good look at my surroundings. But my body refused to obey me. I wanted to push with my legs, but somehow they didn't seem to be getting the instructions. I could see them outlined beneath the covers, but they lay motionless when I told them to move.

"What am I doing here?" I croaked through the pain in my throat. "What happened?"

"You were in an accident," Curly-hair said. "Do you remember anything about it?"

In bits and patches, Friday night came back to me. "We were going to Cori's," I said. "Only—it's so weird—I don't remember the party."

"You were in an accident on the way," Curly-hair explained. "But don't worry. You're going to be fine."

My throat hurt too much for talking, and I was too tired to think. I closed my eyes and tried to find my raft again, to float away from the beeps and the clatter and the strange feeling that my body was no longer my own.

Time had no meaning. It was hard to tell the dreams of sleep from my waking nightmares. At times I woke to find Mom or Dad sitting beside my bed. Their faces looked pale and haggard, but they put on bright smiles when they saw that I was aware of their presence. "Why is my throat so sore?" I asked Mom the first time I discovered her beside me.

"They had a tube down your throat," she said, looking away. "To help you breathe."

"Was I in a coma or something?" I asked.

"You were unconscious for four days," she said. "But you're going to be okay."

If I was going to be okay, why were people always poking and prodding me, jabbing me with needles, and turning me this way and that? Sometimes they pounded me with questions. "Can you feel this? Does that hurt?" they'd ask, pressing here and there on my legs and feet. No, I told them. It didn't hurt. I didn't feel a thing.

Sometimes they gave me orders to follow. "Sit up, Amber," a nurse would command. "Try to move your right foot. . . . Now your left one. .

. . Now, can you wiggle your toes for me? Concentrate! One, two, three . . . "

It should have been so simple. But I watched my thin bare feet as though they belonged to someone else. *One, two, three*, I counted obediently. My toes never even twitched. "When are they going to start moving like normal?" I'd ask. "I've got to get better so I can go home!" But the nurses only shook their heads and told me to be patient. "You were in a very serious accident," they'd say. "Give yourself time."

As I managed to stay awake for longer stretches, my questions grew more insistent. I wanted to know what was wrong with me, and I wanted the details of the accident that had brought me here. One day, when Mom found me sitting up and alert, she explained what had happened. "It seems Eric was speeding," she said grimly. "He was trying to pass the boys in another car, and he missed the curve. He went right off the road into a tree. The door popped open, and you fell out."

A lump of fear rose in my chest. I had to ask the question. "Is Eric okay?"

Mom nodded. "All he got were a few scrapes," she said. "They didn't even keep him overnight."

For an instant, relief washed over me. Eric was alive, not even hurt! I didn't have to worry about him. Then I saw the monstrous injustice of what had happened. "He was the one speeding! And I'm the one stuck in the hospital!" I burst out. "It isn't fair!"

"No, it isn't," Mom agreed. "He's terribly upset. So is his whole family."

"You've talked to them?" I asked. Somehow it hadn't occurred to me before.

"For the insurance settlement." Mom sighed, and her shoulders sagged.

"Insurance?" I said, puzzled. "They're going to pay for the hospital and everything?"

"Don't worry about that part," Mom said. "The only thing you need to think about is getting better."

"When will that be?" I demanded. "How much longer is it going to take?"

Again Mom sighed. She turned to look down the hall, as if she didn't want to face me directly. "I don't know," she said. "We just take it one day at a time. See what the doctors have to say. I don't know."

One day Curly-hair bent over my bed and announced, "You're getting off I.C.U. We're moving you today."

"Where to?" I asked.

"D-4," she said. "It's the teen ward. You'll love it!"

I couldn't imagine loving any ward at Hamilton Hospital. But she had stirred my curiosity. "You mean there are other kids in this place? I'm not the only one?"

"Not by miles," she said, laughing. "You guys are always banging yourselves up!"

"You mean those other kids were all in accidents, too?"

"Some of them, anyway. D-4's got a little of everything. As long as you're between twelve and eighteen, you qualify."

A little later, two orderlies rolled me gently onto a stretcher and wheeled me into the corridor. I'd been in the I.C.U. for two weeks, according to the nurses. For two weeks I had been lost among the glaring lights and beeping machines. Now even the branching hallways, cluttered with racks and wheelchairs and hurrying people, felt like a wider world. I twisted my head from side to side like an eager tourist, trying to take in all the sights as they swept past. A mother pushed twin strollers and carried another baby in a backpack; a bearded young man leaned on a cane and sipped a McDonald's milkshake; two women mopped the floor. In the elevator, a man and woman stepped back to make room for me. They stood holding hands, tears streaming down their cheeks. *What was their story?* I wondered. *What terrible grief did they share?*

My new room was halfway down the hall, across from a stairwell. From my bed by the door I could look out at the passersby. After the I.C.U., D-4 was wonderfully quiet. At the same time, I had a sense of life and activity that had been missing on Intensive Care. As I lay in my high hospital bed I heard young voices in the corridor, and watched kids my own age as they stepped in and out of my line of sight. Some used aluminum walkers; some rode in wheelchairs; and others were up and running on their own two feet. *That's how I'd be walking pretty soon,* I told myself. I was out of the I.C.U.—that was proof that I was getting better. It couldn't be long before life returned to my legs, and I'd skip from one end of the corridor to the other.

Mom, Dad, and Max arrived as I was finishing supper, propped up in bed with a tray table across my lap. "Yuck! What are they feeding you?" Max demanded. "It smells like somebody's sweaty feet!"

I held up a chunk of grayish meat, speared

on the end of my fork. "After the pureed veggies I was getting on I.C.U.," I told him, "this is filet mignon!"

"This place has you warped!" Max said. "That's not even real food, what you're eating!"

It was good to tease with Max again— another sign that I was recovering. I glanced toward Mom and Dad, inviting them to join in the fun. But they stood at the foot of my bed, their faces tired and drawn.

"Come on, you guys!" I protested. "You don't have to worry about me any more. I'm getting out of here, step by step."

"The head nurse stopped us out there," Dad said, waving toward the door. "She's coming in to talk to us."

Something in his voice made me uneasy. "Talk about what?" I asked.

"About your—your condition," Dad said, as if the words were hard to pronounce. "About where we go from here."

"It's about time," I said. "Over in the I.C.U., they never gave me straight answers."

"This lady shoots from the hip," Mom said. "She said she'll try to tell you anything you want to know."

Mom told me that Mrs. Tynan, my math teacher, had called and asked if she should send my assignments. Max said to tell her I was on the terminal ward so I'd never have to do math homework again. I tried to laugh, but it was suddenly hard to make small talk. We were all waiting for the head nurse, for whatever news she had to bring us.

When she came in at last, I knew why Mom said she'd be direct. "Hi," she said. "I'm Midge Hazeldorf. The kids all call me the Midget, so you may as well, too." She was almost as tall as my father, sturdy and athletic. I could picture her dashing up and down a basketball court, catching the ball in her big, strong hands.

"Mom says you can tell me how much longer I've got to stay here," I said.

"You just got here, and already you want to leave us?" she asked. "You haven't even met the gang yet."

"Who's the gang?"

"The other kids on D-4. They're a good bunch. They love to give me headaches."

The Midget was as evasive as everyone else. I dragged her back to my original question. "How long will I be here?"

"It all depends," she said. "It depends on how you do in rehab."

"They mentioned this rehab to us when she was in the I.C.U.," Dad said. "The doctor told us about an exercise program."

"What else did they tell you folks?" the Midget asked. "How much have they told you about Amber's injuries?"

"It has to do with her spinal cord," Mom said. Her voice had an odd, brittle edge, as if she might start to cry at any moment.

"Do all of you understand what that means?" the Midget asked, and her tone was surprisingly gentle.

"I think . . . " Mom began, and left the thought unfinished.

"Amber," the Midget asked, "what have they told you?"

"Nothing," I said. "Nobody wanted to tell me anything."

The Midget gave me a long, searching look. My heart thudded with a sudden terror, and my hand gripped the metal bedrail as though it were a lifeline. But I had to know the truth, whatever it might be. I looked the Midget straight in the eye and said, "Tell me now."

"Your spinal cord was severed in the accident," she said, her words slow and icy clear. "You are paralyzed from the waist down. You'll need to learn to use a wheelchair."

4

My legs might be paralyzed, but there was nothing wrong with my arms. As the Midget's words echoed in my ears, I gave the tray table a mighty shove and sent it careening across the room. It slammed into the wall with a jangling crash. A glass of juice overturned, and a thin stream dripped onto the floor.

"*I* don't need a wheelchair!" I cried. "They can get me to walk again! I *have* to be able to walk!"

"This is really hard," the nurse said gently. "You need time to take it in."

"I don't have to take it in!" I shot back. "It isn't true!"

She didn't argue. She got some paper towels and wiped the splatters from the linoleum. I turned my fury on Mom and Dad. "Did you know about this?" I demanded. "Were you hiding this all along?"

"The doctor talked to us yesterday," Dad admitted. "But these guys don't know everything. They're wrong half the time, and they hate to admit it."

Max cowered silently by the door, and Mom was crying. I looked away, fighting my own tears. *I wouldn't cry*, I told myself fiercely. The doctors were wrong, just like Dad said. If I started crying I would be giving in to them. I needed to resist, to fight back with all my strength.

"We're talking to other specialists," Dad told me. "We sent your records to a guy in New York who's doing experiments on nerves. Getting them to grow back after they're damaged."

"Let's go to New York then!" I cried. "They can't help me here!"

"Of course you want to check out the possibilities," the Midget said. "But meantime, we *can* help you here at Hamilton."

"How? Teaching me to ride my wheelchair up and down the hall?"

She straightened up and dropped her paper towel into the wastebasket. "There's a lot for you to learn," she said. "Take it one day at a time, okay?"

I ignored her and appealed to my parents instead. "Take me to a different hospital!" I pleaded. "These people don't know what they're doing."

I thought they'd agree with me. I thought Dad would promise to buy tickets for New York, and we would all fly out this afternoon.

But he only looked at me helplessly. Finally Mom wiped her eyes and spoke. "You've got to stay here for now, Pumpkin. You've got to do what they tell you."

I would have held up fine if Mom hadn't pulled out that baby name. When she called me "Pumpkin," the years seemed to melt away. I wasn't sixteen any more, I was a little girl of three. I was helpless and scared, and I couldn't hold back my tears any longer.

Later, when everyone had gone, I lay in the dark and remembered that Friday-night ride with Eric Moore. In my imagination, I heard the doorbell ring and rushed to meet him in my stockinged feet. But this time everything was different. This time I told him I had changed my mind. I said I didn't want to go to Cori's party after all. I'd heard he was a dangerous driver, and I wouldn't get into a car with him if he were the last boy on earth. He tried to argue with me, insisting that we'd have a fantastic time, but I held firm. I knew enough not to trust him, with his slick good looks and his easy laugh! At last he turned away, defeated, and I bounded upstairs to the refuge of my room. . . .

Out in the hall a cart clattered. My door swished open and a nurse came in with a glass of water and two little white pills. I swallowed them without even asking what they were. I was in the hospital, and my mother said I had to do what they told me. "Try to get some sleep," the nurse said cheerfully as she went out.

"I'll try," I said, but I lay awake for a long time, wishing I could rewrite the story of that Friday night. I wished I could erase forever my fateful date with Eric Moore.

In the morning the Midget arrived, all smiles, and helped me change from my hospital gown into a shirt and a pair of tights. When I was dressed, she rolled a wheelchair next to my bed. "Let me show you how to transfer," she said, raising the head of the bed so I sat almost upright. "I've locked the brake so the chair won't roll away. Slide over and put your left hand on the seat."

The chair had a tired, battered look, as though it had spent long years in dutiful service.

The seat cushion was threadbare, the padding on the armrest was mended with tape, and the frame was scratched and dented. I wondered if some kid like me had dented it on purpose. I imagined a girl my age being told to transfer and flying into a rage. She fought and shrieked and tried to kick the wretched chair to pieces.

But something was wrong with that picture. If they were making her get into the wheelchair, she wouldn't be able to kick in anger. Her legs would be like mine—heavy as lead.

"Come on," the Midget coaxed. "One hand on the bed and the other on the seat. Then just lift your bottom and swing over. Here—I'll give you a little boost."

"I'm going to fall!" I cried in panic. I had no control as she hoisted my body off the mattress and settled me into the chair. I watched her slide my feet into paper hospital slippers and arrange them on the footrest. I wanted to say, "Wait! Those are *my* feet! You can't just put them where you want them!" But I kept my mouth shut. Do what they tell you to do, Mom had said.

The Midget kept up a one-way conversation as she wheeled me down the hall to the elevator. "You'll be going down to rehab every morning for two hours," she explained. "And in the afternoons, the physiotherapist will come up and work with you on the ward. The idea is for you to be independent. You need to learn to get in and out of your chair. They'll teach you to move in all kinds of situations."

"What situations?" I asked, as the elevator doors slid closed behind us.

"Oh, your house, the mall, school, wherever you want to go."

"Forget it," I said. "I'm not going out in public like this."

"No, I should think not!" she said, eyeing my tights. "You'll have to put some proper clothes on first!"

"You know what I mean," I muttered. "I'm not going out in this thing."

"You're going to hear a lot of talk about adjustment," the Midget said. "After you leave here, life goes on."

We emerged from the elevator on the basement level, and the Midget pushed me down another long corridor. The door marked REHABILITATION was designed with an electric eye, like the door to a supermarket. It glided open as we approached, the way a supermarket door opens for customers with loaded shopping carts.

I felt like a bag of groceries myself when the Midget rolled me toward a bearded, muscular guy in his mid-twenties. She parked me beside him and stepped back. "Amber, this is Carlos," she said. "Carlos, this is Amber Novak, your new patient from D-4."

If I had been standing, Carlos would have been about my height—five-six. Now he loomed above me, leaning down to speak at my level. "Hi, Amber," he said. "Good to see you." He waved toward a series of mats spread in the middle of the room. A girl in shorts lay on one of them, doing exercises. "Go introduce yourself to Amy," Carlos said. "I'll get you started, soon as I do some paperwork here."

I waited for the Midget to give me another push, but when I glanced over my shoulder she was heading for the door. "I'll pick you up in a couple of hours," she called. "Have a good time."

I'd never thought of the Midget as an ally, but I felt abandoned the moment she left. I looked toward Carlos for help, but he was bent over his computer, rattling away at the keyboard. I watched the girl called Amy. Slowly she lifted and lowered one leg, then the other. I felt a surge of hope. Maybe Carlos would teach me to do that, too. If I could only move my legs, I'd learn to walk again somehow. I'd show them I didn't need their stupid, ugly wheelchair!

With a last sidelong glance at Carlos, I pressed my hands to the wheels of my chair and propelled it forward. It moved with surprising ease, and in moments I arrived at the mats. For the first time in weeks, I had moved of my own free will.

Amy let her leg flop to the mat. "Hi," she panted, lifting up on her elbows to look at me.

Glancing past her, I noticed a set of parallel bars, a stationary bicycle, and a collection of other equipment at the far end of the room. "Do you get to use all that stuff?" I asked her.

"The rack, the iron maiden, the thumb screw—take your pick," she said.

"It's that bad?"

"Well, it's not a trip to the beach," Amy said. Two dimples appeared on her cheek when she smiled, and I decided I was going to like her.

"I don't care if it's torture," I blurted out. "I can take it, if it'll get me out of this chair!"

"You want a change of scene, is that it?" Carlos asked, striding over to me. "I'm going to get you busy with some passive movement."

He lifted me from my chair as though I were weightless, and set me lightly down on the mat next to Amy's. Crouching by my feet, he began to move my legs, bending and straightening, lifting them up and down. As he set my right leg down, it began to twitch and jump as though it were trying to dance. "Why does that happen?" I asked. "I can't make it stop!"

"You want to know how smart your brain is?" Carlos asked. "Okay, here goes. Your brain knows you can't control your legs since your accident. But it knows they need exercise. So it still manages to send signals down there every now and then. 'Move! Get that circulation going! Don't just laze around all day!'"

I was not impressed. "Great," I said. "When's my brain going to wake up and listen to me?"

"The trouble isn't in your head, it's in your spinal cord," Carlos said patiently. "You know how the spinal cord works? Did they explain it to you?"

"They said it was—severed," I told him. It was hard to say the word. It sounded so complete, so final.

"The brain is kind of like the central computer," Carlos said. "It's wired up to every part of your body, sending out messages, getting messages back. All those messages, they go down the spinal cord that's inside your backbone. They branch out along thousands of nerves that go everywhere, from your toes to your eyebrows."

Carlos shifted his attention for a moment to Amy. "Move it, girl!" he exclaimed. "You've got work to do!" Amy sighed and went back to her leg lifts.

"I can move my head and shoulders and arms fine," I pondered. "How come I can't get my legs to work yet?"

"It depends on where the spinal cord is injured," Carlos said. "See, the nerves that branch out from the upper part, they control the upper part of your body. The nerves that fan out lower down, they control your legs and feet. So if you've got a break lower down, then your brain tells your feet to move, but the message doesn't get through."

"Those twitch messages get through, though," I protested. "Why not the rest?"

"There are probably a few wispy little connections left," Carlos said. "But you've got to work with what you've got."

"You mean I can use those little wisps and get my legs stronger?"

He shook his head. "You can strengthen your upper body and get it to really work for you."

That wasn't the answer I wanted, but it was all Carlos was willing to offer. After my "passive movement" session, he put me on a padded table with a metal frame above me. I had to reach up, grasp the frame, and pull myself into a sitting position. It wasn't as easy as it sounded. It was hard to balance when my legs just lay there inertly, refusing to help.

As I worked at my sit-ups, the rehab room began to fill with people. A physiotherapist named Angie came in with two boys, Aaron and Jack. They seemed to be old friends. Aaron teased Jack about his big feet, and Jack gave Aaron's wheelchair a playful shove. When he spoke, Jack sounded as if someone was hanging on to the end of his tongue. I couldn't catch most of what he said, but Aaron understood him perfectly when he tossed out his next insult.

"Save it for later," Angie told them, laughing. "You guys have work to do first."

"Hey, Amy, who's your friend?" Aaron asked. "You going to introduce us?"

"She can talk," Amy said. "She can introduce herself if she wants."

"Do you want?" Aaron asked me. I never would have expected to meet a cute guy in rehab, but Aaron proved me wrong.

"I'm Amber," I said. "I'm new."

"So how do you like Old Alice?" he asked.

"Old Alice?" I repeated. "Who's that?"

"Alice Hamilton. Old Alice, I call her."

I giggled. "Is there really such a person?" I wondered aloud.

"Used to be," Amy said. "Alice Hamilton was a doctor about a hundred years ago. She went around cleaning up the slums because too many people were getting TB and things like that."

"So how do you like Old Alice?" Aaron asked again. "What's your honest opinion?"

"How can I like it?" I demanded. "I don't want to be here. I wish none of this had ever happened."

Jack spoke up. I didn't understand much of what he said, but Amy translated. "You're one of us now," she told me. She glanced at Jack to be sure she was getting it right, and added, "Like it or not, you're here."

5

~~~

Sometimes Mom and Dad took turns coming to see me on D-4. At other times they arrived together. Whenever they brought Max along, he scuffed his feet restlessly, hands in his pockets and eyes downcast. "I hate this place," he burst out one day. "I wish I'd never have to see this hospital for the rest of my life!"

"That makes two of us!" I said fervently.

Max smiled, a little embarrassed. "I don't hate seeing *you*," he tried to assure me. "It's the hospital I can't stand! I can't even stand the way it smells!"

I sniffed. "I don't smell anything," I said. "What are you talking about?"

"It smells like medicine, and yucky cafeteria food, and that stuff they clean the floors with,"

Max said. "How do you stand it all the time?"

"I don't even notice it anymore," I said. "This is scary! I've lived here so long it's starting to feel normal."

It was true. My life at Hamilton Hospital had slipped into a routine that was almost comfortable. Every day was built around a predictable schedule of meals, medications, and exercises. When I got a bit of free time, I wheeled myself down to the lounge and hung out with Amy, Jack, Aaron, and the other kids on the teen ward. Amy and I talked about school and our friends back home, but that world seemed farther and farther away. Our real world was right here, small and safe. We played video games, watched movies, flirted with the boys. If I had to be stuck in a wheelchair for a while, D-4 wasn't a bad place to pass the time.

I was heading to the lounge one afternoon, ready to relax after an hour of pull-ups and arm swings, when a vaguely familiar figure stepped from the elevator. The hair wasn't quite what I remembered, which made the whole face look rounder and fuller. But when I caught a glimpse of that bulging green backpack, the whole picture fell into place. "Katrina?" I asked in wonder.

"I told you I'd come see you," she reminded me. "Did you forget?"

"I didn't expect you today," I stammered. "It feels strange to see you here."

If I hadn't been in the wheelchair I would have rushed to give her a hug. Now she stood tall and awkward beside me. I was too close to the floor. The metal frame and the patched arm-rests were in the way.

An orderly approached with a cartload of dirty linen. "We're blocking the hall," I told Katrina. "Come on down to my room, where we can talk."

My room gave us a bit of privacy, but I still felt a sense of distance between us. Katrina perched on the edge of a straight-backed chair, leaning forward as if she were ready to jump up and flee. Neither of us mentioned my wheel-chair, but she kept staring at it and glancing away again. "So what's new at school?" I asked, to nudge the conversation along.

She looked relieved, and poured out a flood of stories. "Maura Shehan broke up with that guy Joe—you know, that big slob with the loud voice? Robin Kozlowski and Christa Morton had a fight in the girls' locker room after P.E., and nobody knows what it was about. And Mark

Spangler broke his ankle Rollerblading. He's hobbling around on crutches and everybody calls him Crip. . . . "

She trailed off, stricken. "I'm sorry," she gasped. "I didn't mean it like—you know—"

"It's okay," I said quickly. "You didn't hurt my feelings."

"Still," she said, "I should be more—you know—more aware." She drummed her toes on the floor, itching to be gone.

"Thank everybody for the get-well cards," I said. "And all the flowers. Look, Cori Madison sent me that plant on the windowsill."

"Neat," Katrina said, hardly glancing at it. "I'll tell her you've got it."

"And my brother brought those," I added, gesturing toward a bowl on my nightstand where a pair of goldfish swam in endless circles.

"Oh," she said. "Nice." There was a long, painful pause. A question rose up in my mind. I tried to squash it down but it wouldn't go away. "What are they saying back there?" I asked. "About the accident? About me?"

"Everybody's in shock," Katrina said. "You're a regular kid, like the rest of us. How could you end up in a wheelchair?"

"What else?" I pressed. "What do they say about the accident?"

"It was Eric's fault," Katrina said, and her voice had a bitter edge. "They tried to keep his name out of the papers because he's under eighteen, but everybody knows he was going too fast."

I hadn't thought about the newspapers. But in a town like ours, my story would have been a front-page headline. "I guess they didn't want me to read about it," I said. "Maybe they thought I'd get upset."

"Upset!" Katrina exclaimed, and for the first time her laugh sounded utterly genuine. "You spend four days in a coma, you're sitting in a wheelchair, who knows how much longer you'll be stuck in the hospital—and they think a newspaper might upset you! What?"

I had to laugh, too. I couldn't help it. It was the first time I'd managed to find a glimmer of humor in my situation, and the feeling was wonderful.

But it only lasted a moment. Into the quiet between us Katrina announced, "He wants to come see you."

"Who does?" I demanded, as if I didn't know.

"Eric. He told me to ask you."

My heart thundered inside my chest. My whole body tensed, and even my usually silent toes seemed to tingle. "What does he want?" I asked, and heard the tremble in my voice.

"To tell you he's sorry, I guess."

"Sorry!" I cried. "Is that all? Eric Moore is sorry?"

"Of course he is!" Katrina protested. "He didn't do it on purpose! He feels awful!"

"Sorry is what you say when you step on somebody's toe!" I said, my words tumbling out of control. "You say sorry when you tip over somebody's Coke, or spill catsup on somebody's math book! How does he think he can make up for this by saying he's sorry!"

I stopped, breathless. No words were strong enough to capture my anger and my pain. And no words could ever make up for what Eric had done to my life.

"You should see him." Katrina was almost pleading with me. "He never smiles any more. He hardly says a word."

"What can he say?" I asked bitterly. "I'd be quiet, too, if I were him!"

"Yeah, but I feel bad for him sometimes," Katrina said. "He walks around like a zombie!"

"At least he walks," I said. "What's he got to complain about?"

"Okay," said Katrina. "Should I say you don't want to see him?"

"I don't want to see him ever again!" I said.

For another second I managed to hold back my tears. Then they burst forth on a torrent of words. "I don't want to hear his voice! I don't want to think about him! I wish I could just erase him from the world! Tell him that, Katrina! Tell him that from me!"

I didn't want to think about Eric Moore, but after Katrina left, I couldn't push him out of my mind. I wondered if people asked him about the accident, and how he answered their questions. I imagined kids staring at him and whispering. Did he admit that he'd been racing the guys in the other car? Did he explain he'd been showing off, acting like a first-class jerk?

He was sorry, he said. Sorry wouldn't get me out of this wheelchair. Sorry wouldn't bring life back to my legs.

How did he dare? I thought, pounding the armrests. How did he dare to ask to see me? *How did he dare believe sorry could be enough?*

6

———

Slowly, out on the edge of my awareness, May faded into June. When people came in from out-doors, their faces were flushed and they moaned about the unbearable heat. But on D-4 the tem-perature never altered. All I knew of the world outside was the view of Lake Michigan from the window at the end of the corridor.

Max began his summer vacation. He told me about trips to the pool, about shooting bas-kets in the park, and running through the sprin-kler. The next time Katrina came to visit, her sunburned nose was peeling, while the rest of her had darkened to a golden tan. She wouldn't be back for a while, she explained; she was going to Colorado to stay with her cousins in the mountains. I was going nowhere. I was spending my summer on D-4 at Hamilton Hospital.

My teachers sent me folders of assignments. They wrote friendly notes, encouraging me to get well soon and assuring me that I could catch up on all the work I had missed. I added homework to my daily routine. I spread my books on a table in the lounge and worked math problems or wrote essays amid the din. Most days Jack's music pounded from the CD player and Aaron, Amy and the others played video games. I was among friends. We didn't talk much about the accidents and diseases that brought us to Old Alice. We talked about which nurses were mean and which ones we could con into letting us have visitors past eight o'clock. We talked about our favorite bands and movies. Amy confessed that she had a crush on Carlos, and I reminded her that he wore a wedding ring.

One day Aaron tuned in on our conversation. "What do you care about one of those stilt-walkers for?" he teased. "They look like a gust of wind could topple them over."

"Stilt-walkers!" I exclaimed. "Who calls them that?"

"I do," said Aaron, with a glint of mischief. "I look at people walking around on their tall, skinny legs and it doesn't make sense. How do they balance?"

"Hey! I'm part stilt-walker myself," said Amy. "I can do the vertical thing on crutches. The chair's a lot faster, though."

"How much faster?" I asked. I was startled by the mischief in my own voice. Aaron's tone was contagious.

"Fast!" said Amy. "Just give me room to zoom!"

Aaron wheeled to the doorway and peered out. "Plenty of room out there," he reported. "Who's up for a race?"

Within moments the three of us had lined up side by side at the end of the corridor. "On your mark!" Aaron cried. "Get set! Go!"

I put my hands to the wheels and gave a mighty thrust. But already Amy was speeding ahead of me, with Aaron only a foot behind her. *I wouldn't be left in the dust*, I told myself fiercely. I pushed harder and my chair surged forward. Aaron edged toward the middle of the hall, blocking my way. I couldn't pass him, and Amy raced yards in front. As I tried to maneuver past Aaron, my footrest slammed into the side of his chair and both of us came to a crashing halt.

"Beat you!" Amy called back, laughing.

"Aaron cheated!" I said. We were all laughing now. "He got in my way on purpose!"

"Hey, keep it down, you guys!" ordered the Midget, emerging from the nurses' station. "What's going on out here, anyway?"

"The hundred-yard crash," said Aaron, and we went into gales of laughter again.

What would the kids back at school think of my new friends? I wondered. *For that matter, what would they think of me?* I was in no hurry to find out. As long as I had to use a wheelchair, I preferred to stay safe on D-4, where I was one of the gang.

I could never understand what Amy saw in Carlos. To me, he was the enemy. He worked me relentlessly in rehab for hours each day. I swung from rings, lifted weights, and rolled and tumbled on the mats. "To build upper-body strength," as he put it, I leaned on a bench-press. By the beginning of July I could hitch my way forward between the parallel bars, my feet trailing beneath me along the floor. It felt strange and frightening to stand upright after sitting for so long. I looked at Carlos eye to eye, and he didn't have to bend down to speak to me. I was up and moving on the bars, but I wasn't walking.

My legs hung like sandbags, and my feet flopped loosely on my ankles. My arms and shoulders throbbed with effort as I propelled myself between the bars, hand over hand. I ordered my legs to help, but time after time they ignored my commands. They tingled, they ached, sometimes they twitched, but they never did anything I told them to do.

The people at Hamilton were dedicated to teaching me everything I needed for my new life. The occupational therapist showed me how to pull loose-fitting pants up my motionless legs, how to take a shower sitting on a plastic stool. From Carlos I learned to transfer from my chair to the seat of an automobile. But I didn't want to learn to live from a wheelchair. I wanted my old life back again, as if the accident had never happened.

My frustration boiled over one afternoon when Dad dropped by on his way home from work. "They're not helping me in here!" I exploded. "When are you going to move me to a better hospital?"

Dad stood up and paced to the window. "You know we've been talking to other doctors," he said. "We sent your records all over—California, New York, Boston—"

I pounced on the words "New York." "What about that experimental program? The one where they get the nerves to grow again!"

His shoulders sagged. "We got a letter from those people yesterday. What they're doing is only a study, you know. It's still in the very early stages. They say you don't qualify."

"What do you mean? I'm in a wheelchair! I've got a spinal-cord injury! Their whole study's about people like me."

"It's more complicated than that," Dad explained. "In this project, they have to give you some kind of special injection within twenty-four hours of your injury. Otherwise, it's too late."

"So I might have had a chance?" I cried. "Why don't they do that injection here? I hate this stupid hospital! I hate it!"

"Hamilton is top of the line," Dad said. "That's what everyone keeps telling us."

I didn't want to hear it. "What about Boston then? Or California? There's got to be some-place better than this dump!"

"We're doing the best we can," Dad said brusquely. "We're not magicians, you know!"

"Okay," I said. "But what am I supposed to do? I can't go through life like this!"

"You're alive," Dad said. "You've got a good mind. We've got a lot to be thankful for."

"Thankful!" I exclaimed. "I'm stuck in the hospital while everybody else is at the beach! While everybody else runs around playing Frisbee, I'm sitting in this wheelchair!"

Dad paced from the window to the door. He hated tears, but today he was kind enough to let me cry. "We won't give up," he promised. "We'll do everything possible."

"Please," I begged, "please don't give up on me. If you and Mom give up, I don't know what I'll do!"

"This is the twenty-first century," Dad said, straightening his shoulders. "There's got to be someone who can help you walk again."

I felt stronger and braver after Dad left that afternoon. *It couldn't be much longer now*, I told myself. *They'd get me out of Hamilton and send me to a proper hospital*. Dad was right—this was the twenty-first century. Human beings cloned sheep and sent cameras to Mars. Surely someone could mend a broken spinal cord.

My mind leaped ahead to the day I'd come back for a visit to D-4. I'd stride through the door and march up to the nurses' station. No one would recognize the new, vertical me. At last one of the nurses would say, "Amber? Amber Novak?" with wonder in her voice. "It's me!" I'd tell her, breaking into a grin. "You didn't think I could do it, did you? Wait till I show Carlos! Wait till I show Amy and Aaron and all the gang! . . . "

The fantasy faded. I sat in my wheelchair in my hospital room, the walls covered with cards from well-wishers. Would I ever leave this tiny cubicle that had become my home? Would I ever have a real life at all?

The summer wore on, one day blending into the next. Dad sent my medical records here and there, and talked to doctors and researchers at one hospital after another. The answers were monotonous. "Alice Hamilton is one of the finest hospitals in the country. You can't do better than to have your daughter treated there." "Nerve regeneration? There are some promising results with mice. . . . Maybe in another five or ten years . . . " "With good rehabilitation, your daughter will be able to lead a nearly normal life."

Sometimes truth comes in one moment of blazing clarity. But that's not how it happened for me that summer at Hamilton. My new reality seeped in little by little with each passing day. Every time Dad reported another doctor's letter or another discouraging phone call from some far-away clinic, my certainty grew. I found myself working harder during my sessions in rehab. This was my opportunity to build my strength, to learn the things I needed to know. My wheelchair was part of my future, part of my life forever.

In August Carlos started to slip the words "going home" into our conversations. "You'll probably need to rearrange the furniture when you go home," he said one day. "Make sure you've got clear pathways for crossing rooms." Another time he said, "I've got some pamphlets for your parents, about putting in ramps and widening doorways."

I looked up at him from the mat, where he had me doing push-ups. "They can't tear the house apart for me!" I protested. "I can't ask them to do that!"

"Well," he said evenly, "you won't like being trapped in one little room, will you? When you go home, I think you'd rather live in your whole house."

"What I really want when I go home," I said, "is to walk up the front steps."

Carlos shook his head. "You ever hear that

old song by the Rolling Stones?" he asked. "It says 'You can't always get what you want.'"

"I think I've heard it," I said. "It has a chorus singing those lines, right?"

"That's the one," said Carlos. "And it says if you try real hard, you'll get what you need."

I glanced over at Amy, who was hopping along on a pair of crutches. "If she can walk, so can I," I declared.

"Get real, girl!" Carlos said. "Amy's not you, and you're not Amy! She's got a problem with her hips. You have a spinal-cord injury, don't forget!"

No one spoke to me that way. People were gentle and sympathetic when they talked to me. They understood that I was miserable, and they tried to help me feel better. Carlos had no right to tell me to "get real," as if I were whining for attention like a spoiled brat.

With every fiber of my being I longed to leap up and flee from the room. But even now my legs refused to obey me. My wheelchair was parked a few feet away, my only means of escape. I could crawl to it and hoist myself into the seat. I could wheel out of the gym and take the elevator back to D-4. But it wouldn't be the swift, dramatic exit I yearned for.

Instead of fleeing, I'd find a different way to fight back. "I *am* being real," I told Carlos quietly. "I'm going to have the kind of life I need and want. I'll show you."

"I hope you will," he said. "We've put a lot of work in. I want to see results."

7

To my dismay, Aaron went home one day in August. Amy was discharged by the end of the same week. Jack was scheduled to leave the first of September. "They try to get us out in time for school," he explained in his slow, labored voice. By now I understood him easily, without a second thought—and it was almost time to say good-bye.

New kids came onto D-4 as my old friends disappeared, but I kept my distance. I didn't want to make new friends, only to lose them again. My own time on the ward was running out.

The Midget brought me the fateful news one afternoon as I emerged from the elevator after a workout in the pool. "Hey Amber," she said brightly. "We're going to miss you around here."

"What do you mean?" I asked, dazed.

She laughed. "Didn't anyone tell you? Dr. Mann just handed me your paperwork. You go home on Saturday."

One thing about using a wheelchair—when you feel a wave of dizziness wash over you, you're already sitting down. "Not *this* Saturday!" I exclaimed. "I'm not ready yet!"

"What are you waiting for?" she asked.

It was one of those questions that doesn't deserve an answer, and I didn't offer one. "Listen," she said more gently, "I know it's a big change. Come to the teen group tomorrow. Some of your buddies will be there. You can hear how it's going for them."

The Midget had been nudging me to attend her teen discussion group ever since I came to D-4. I sat in once or twice, but I always felt restless and out of place. Most of the kids in the group had diseases, such as lupus or diabetes or cancer—illnesses that might kill them, or at best would hang on for years. I felt that their issues had nothing to do with mine. I wasn't sick; I had been in an accident. That was very different.

Now they were sending me home in a wheelchair. How would I navigate through the world sitting down? It was unthinkable, despite all my work with Carlos and the others. But somehow I would have to begin, this Saturday.

I wouldn't be the first. Others had done it before me. Maybe they could give me pointers that would be of use. I was going to need all the help I could get.

To my delight, Aaron was there to greet me when I wheeled into the lounge at three the next afternoon. "I never thought I'd be so glad to see the inside of this place again," he said when he caught sight of me. "It's looking a whole lot better than I remembered."

"How come?" I asked.

"Electric-eye doors," he said. "These nice, wide hallways with no steps. Elevators every-where! I *love* elevators!"

This was not encouraging. It was not what I wanted to hear. "Carlos has been talking to my parents about fixing up the house for me," I told him. "They put in a ramp so I can get up to the front door."

"One ramp," Aaron said with a shrug. "Well, you've got to start somewhere."

Before I could ask him what he meant, the Midget came in and shut the door. The room fell suddenly quiet. I glanced around at the other kids sitting on chairs and sofas. I recognized a girl named Melissa, who had been in for a few weeks last May. Most of the others were new to me. They must all be "outpatients," people who had been discharged but came back to see a doctor or get some sort of treatment such as physical therapy. I wondered if I would hurry back here, as Aaron had. Would I be overwhelmed away from Hamilton, in a world of stilt-walkers?

Slow seconds ticked by. I glanced from face to face, wishing someone would break the silence. At last the Midget spoke. "Ah, summer!" she sighed. "The good old summertime! You guys ready to go back to school yet?"

Everyone groaned on cue. To my surprise, Aaron said proudly, "I just joined the working world. I sort jars at the recycling center."

Back in the old days, before the accident, I might have thought that was a job for a loser. Now I leaned toward him and whispered, "That's cool! You didn't tell me you found a summer job!" If I didn't get back on my feet, I thought, would anyone ever hire me? Would I have Aaron's determination and good luck?

Other kids talked about the work they'd been doing all summer. A girl named Chloe, who looked perfectly healthy to me, said she put in three mornings a week at an animal shelter. Another girl, Cassie, told a long, complicated story about being a counselor at a camp for kids with diabetes. She didn't tell the other counselors that she had diabetes herself, and wound up getting really sick. She tried to blame it all on her mother for not trusting her to take care of herself.

"You get yourself sick because you're mad at your mom?" Aaron asked. "That makes a lot of sense!"

I could hardly believe what I was hearing. Was this the same fun-loving Aaron who was a whiz at Nintendo, who flirted with me and Amy, who loved to buck hospital rules? This was a side of him I'd never seen before.

Cassie glared at him. I wanted to soften Aaron's words, to get the idea across in a way that wouldn't have such a bite to it. "That's what happens when you're really mad sometimes," I said. "You end up taking it out on yourself."

"You think so?" Cassie asked. "That's weird, isn't it?"

"It's weird, but it's human nature," the Midget put in.

That comment turned the talk toward

weirdness for a while. A boy named Howard claimed that we were all mutants. The Midget said we were "standard-issue teenagers," that we were all weird in normal ways.

"That's not what most people think," Aaron said grimly. "They see you in a wheelchair and something in their head goes *click!* Look out, there's a weirdo heading this way."

"Oh, they're not mean on purpose," said Chloe, the animal-shelter girl. "They just get— you know—scared when they're around somebody who's different from them."

"Yeah? Then how come they call you things like 'crip' and 'gimp'?" Aaron demanded. "They say stuff like that to you, it's not exactly friendly."

I shrank down in my chair, wishing I could become invisible. No wonder Aaron came back to Hamilton the first chance he got! He knew what was out there. He knew what was waiting for me.

"Sticks and stones will break my bones," Howard chanted with a generous portion of sarcasm, "but names will never hurt me."

"Ha!" said Melissa, who used a crutch when she walked. "Whoever made that one up lived in a cocoon."

The way she said the word "cocoon" made

everybody laugh. It helped to break the tension. I found myself sitting up tall again.

"Hey, let's not go nuts on PC," commented Latisha, who sat next to Chloe. "People can take it too far, you know."

"Like calling her the Midget," Howard said, pointing. "Maybe that's an insult, huh?"

I thought about it. "Someone who's really short might not like it," I said. "I mean, they might hear us talk about the Midget and feel like we're making fun of people who are small."

"You know, I haven't given this a lot of thought myself," the Midget said. "People have called me Midget all my life, just because my name is Midge."

"Plus you're really in the *non*-midget category," Howard added. "To be PC about it."

"For me it's just—what people call me around here," the Midget went on. "Only 'midget' gets put on some people as a label. Labels are pretty hurtful."

"Okay, so what are you supposed to call some lady who's three feet tall?" Latisha asked.

"How about Jane," the Midget said. "Or Mary. Or whatever her name is."

"Do we have to change what we call you?" Howard asked in astonishment.

"I'm not sure I'm ready for this!" the Midget said. "Talk about a challenge!"

"We could call you Hazel," Aaron suggested. "Midge Hazeldorf. Hazel."

"Sounds like somebody's maid," said Chloe. "'Hazel, bring me another cup of tea!'"

"That's me all right," the Midget laughed. "All day long, bring this, get that!"

"This is why I wanted to come back here today," Aaron said with a sigh. "In here you can talk about anything. It's so, so easy!"

"And out there it's not?" I asked him.

He shook his head. "Out there it can get rough sometimes," he said. "That's the truth. Sometimes it's not easy at all."

On Friday, the day before I was due to go home, Katrina paid me a final hospital visit. She was growing used to my wheelchair, and most of the tension between us had melted away. We sat in the lounge as kids drifted in and out, some walking and some riding. Katrina was filled with stories about her Colorado summer. She told me about hikes in the mountains, parties with her cousins' friends, and a long ride on horseback over a remote trail. I listened with a strange mixture of pleasure and sadness. It was wonderfully refreshing to hear about Katrina's adventures, to imagine a life of fun and freedom far from the halls of Hamilton. I was glad that Katrina had enjoyed her summer so much, and glad that she came to share it with me. Still, it hurt to know I would not be able to hike those trails beside her. If I went to one of those parties I wouldn't be seen as interesting or pretty or fun. I'd only be "the girl in the wheelchair." As for horseback riding—my mind veered away from the thought. In my new life, how could any of those things be within my reach?

"Amber," Katrina said, and I heard a note of caution in her voice. "Amber—I've got something for you."

"It doesn't exactly sound like a present," I said, suddenly on guard.

She rummaged in her pocketbook. "It's a letter. I'm supposed to give it to you."

"A letter from who?" I had the feeling I knew already.

Without a word, Katrina handed me the plain white envelope. I took it gingerly, as if it might burn my fingertips. My hands shook as I drew out the single folded sheet.

● ● ●

Dear Amber,

I have a lot to say to you, and I can't do it very well in a letter. You probably don't ever want to hear from me again, and I don't blame you for that! Still, it would mean so much to me if we could at least try to talk. It's asking a lot, I know, but I've been thinking about you for so long, and I need to say some things to you in person.

May I call you when you get home from the hospital? I really hope you say yes.

Sincerely,
Eric

"Amber?" Katrina said anxiously.

I opened my eyes. They were filled with tears. I thought of Eric, Eric the linebacker, Eric the center of every crowd—Eric Moore struggling to write the letter I clutched in my trembling hand. I thought of him searching for just the right words, and asking so humbly if I would talk to him. He asked nothing more than that— just a chance to speak to me.

Then my pain and anger rose up again. Why should I be sorry for Eric? Of course he felt pangs of conscience. His sorrow didn't erase what he had done to me. Nothing he said could undo that Friday night of Cori's party.

I handed the letter back to Katrina. She read it swiftly. "Give the guy a chance!" she said. "You've got to talk to him after he writes a letter like that!"

"No, I don't," I said. "He's had his chance, and he messed up. Big time!"

8

Packing to leave the hospital took more time and effort than I had expected. Mom and Dad had brought more and more of my things from home each time they came to see me—shirts and sweaters, makeup, conditioner, my CD player and most of my CDs, books, magazines, my giant stuffed Simba from *The Lion King*. That final week Dad brought me a suitcase and a stack of empty cardboard boxes. I put off packing as long as I could. On Friday night, when I finally got started, I discovered it took a lot longer than I expected. It was hard to maneuver in that cramped little room, cluttered with nightstand, tray table, and extra chairs for visitors. If I wheeled up to the cupboard at the end of my bed, the footrest got in the way and I couldn't get the door open. To pull the photos and posters from the wall I had to transfer from my chair to the bed and lean on one hand for balance while I peeled tape with the other. Nothing was within easy reach. Everything was in the way of everything else. I was ready to snap someone's head off. When the nurse formerly known as the Midget walked in, she got the full gale of my frustration.

"This is impossible!" I exploded. "I can't do it anymore! I'm sick of trying!"

"Oh, heck, I forgot my magic wand," she said. "I could wave it and tell all your clothes to fold themselves up and float into your suitcase."

"It's not funny!" I raged at her. "The simplest thing takes forever in this stupid chair! I hate it! I really, really hate it!"

"I hear you," she said. "It's a big change. You're still going through the transition. It'll get easier as you go along."

"Nothing gets easier!" I rushed on. "And it's going to be even harder when I get home! You heard what Aaron said!"

"Some things will be hard for a while," she agreed. "Still, what's the alternative? Stay in a hospital the rest of your life?"

"And I'm tired of getting advice!" I said. "I'm

sick of advice from—from you stilt-walkers!"

She threw back her head and laughed. "Sticks and stones will break my bones," she chanted. "You're right. What do we stilt-walkers know?"

Somehow her laughter took the edge off my fury. I sprawled on the bed and let myself laugh, too. "You know a lot about how it is, just from working here," I conceded at last. "You watch us kids. But you don't know from the inside what it's like to go around in a wheelchair."

She nodded. "Neither do you yet, in a way," she said thoughtfully. "You haven't learned the ins and outs. And you haven't really accepted it as part of who you are."

"I can live with it because I have to," I said. "But I'll never accept it! That would be like giving up."

"It's not giving up," she said gently. "It's accepting what you have and who you are. It's being at peace so you can get on with your life."

"Sounds like more advice," I muttered. "I've got to finish packing."

"Go to it," she said. "Those shirts are yelling, 'Fold me!'"

"Midge—" I began, as she turned to go. "I mean—Hazel?"

She looked back, a hand on her hip. "Are you addressing me?" she asked.

"I just want to say—" I gulped and started again. "You've really been nice to me—patient and everything—even when I give you a hard time. I just want to tell you—thank you."

I knew I was blushing by the time I got the words out. *Why is it so embarrassing to thank someone,* I wondered. Everything I said was true. I complained all the time. It must be pretty annoying to listen to me day after day. And the Midget—Hazel—really did try her best. She was the nicest nurse on D-4. She was the one who kept everything together.

"You're very welcome, Amber," she said. "I do mean it. I hope you'll come back and see us."

"Just like Aaron," I said. "I'll retreat back here the first chance I get."

"Not retreat," she said. "Think of it as coming back to bring us a report from the field."

"Whatever," I said, and stretched up for another photo.

The next morning Mom and Dad arrived on D-4 to sign papers and carry my belongings downstairs. I said my last good-byes as quickly as I could. Now that my departure was at hand, I didn't want to linger. I had said everything I had to say, and it was time to be gone.

It felt strange to get off the elevator at "Ground" instead of "Basement." In the lobby, the wheels of my chair sank into the carpet and fought my efforts to move forward. I strained to push the wheels, and rolled slowly to the front door.

"Want a push?" Dad asked.

I shook my head. "No," I said. "I guess I need the practice. Up on D-4, everything's linoleum."

Why didn't they have nice smooth linoleum floors down here in the lobby? I asked myself. Pushing across the carpet felt like wheeling my way through mud. If only I were walking out the front door, instead of riding in this chair! Then I wouldn't give one thought to the carpet. I'd see only the sun pouring through the glass doors, and the car waiting in the parking lot to carry me home at last.

In the parking lot Dad helped me transfer to the front seat. He folded my wheelchair and stowed it in back while Mom rearranged my boxes in the trunk. Finally, we were off.

As we pulled out into traffic, I craned my neck for a final look at the hospital. D-4 lay somewhere in that vast sprawl of roofs and towers. For one piercing moment I longed to rush back to that refuge, with its safe routines and its polished level floors. Then I faced front and thought about going home.

At first, when we stopped in front of the house, I didn't see the ramp. The workmen had built it off to the side, half-obscured by the shrubbery. I was glad people wouldn't see it from the street. I didn't want to announce to the world, "A wheelchair person lives here." Dad set up the chair beside the open door of the car. "Did you lock the brakes?" I asked. "I don't want to go flying."

"They're locked," he assured me. He'd studied this maneuver with Carlos last week, but now we were on our own. It wasn't the same at all.

I looked down, gauging the distance. The seat of the minivan was nearly a foot higher than the seat of my chair. My stomach lurched when I gazed at the gap I needed to swing across. "Need a hand?" Dad asked.

"I think the answer's yes," I said. Dad leaned in and boosted me from the car. With a grunt of effort, he set me down in the wheelchair. My legs draped onto the ground and I bent forward to place my feet on the footrest. The whole maneuver was awkward and slow. When I glanced up I saw old Mr. Reynolds, our neighbor across the street, peering from his front window. Halfway up the block two girls on bikes stopped to stare at me. "What is this, the welcoming committee?" I asked Dad. He didn't laugh. Neither did I.

Mom came up behind me, a box in one hand and a suitcase in the other. "I can help you up the ramp," she said. "Just let me go in and put this stuff down."

"It's okay, I'll help her," Dad said. He took hold of the handles and started to push.

"Wait," I protested. "I need to do it myself. I've got to get the hang of it."

"Suit yourself," Dad said a little brusquely. I rounded the bushes and started up the ramp. It wasn't as steep as some of the inclines I had practiced on down in rehab. But in the heavy afternoon heat it was challenge enough. At each turn of the wheels I gripped hard, trying to use my hands as brakes. If I didn't hang on with all my power, I felt as though I would roll backwards. I might even topple over and land on my head.

"Want me to help?" Dad asked again. I waved him away and struggled higher. "So much for Carlos' upper-body strength," I panted. "This is harder than it looks!"

"I can help . . . " Dad protested, but with a final burst I reached the top and pushed over the tiny threshold at the front door. For the first time in months, I was inside my own house.

The moment I rolled into the front hall I knew it was worth the effort. There was the full-length mirror on the closet door, the umbrella stand heaped with cast-off hats and rain gear, the hanging chimes that sounded the doorbell. I made my way over the edge of the carpet and into the living room. The same Swiss cuckoo clock still hung on the wall, and there was the TV, the bookcases, the fireplace and its mantel filled with knicknacks and trophies. I sat motionless in the middle of the room, fighting back tears as memory swept over me. I was a different person the last time I entered this room. That was so long ago now. Where was that carefree girl who bounded to the door last spring and nearly stepped outside in her stockinged feet? Who was I now—a refugee from D-4, returning like Rip Van Winkle after his long sleep?

Feet thudded overhead, and Max pounded downstairs. He leaped over the two steps at the bottom and jumped straight into the air, hands upraised so that his fingertips grazed the ceiling. "Oh, man!" he said, landing with a flat-footed thump. "I almost did it!"

"Almosts don't count," I said. "Mom, where are you putting my stuff?"

"We've set up your room in the den," Mom said. "Take a look."

Sure enough, when I wheeled into the den, everything was there—my bed, my bureau, my desk and chair. My pictures hung on the walls, and my CD player was set up on the bookcase. They had even hung my curtains on the den's tall windows. They were a little too short, but they were my own.

"Do you like it?" Mom asked anxiously. "You can move things around if you're not happy."

"It's fine," I said. They had done everything they could to make my new room comfortable and familiar. But still, it was the den, dressed up to look like my own private space. It was a public room, just off the dining room. How could it ever really belong to me?

Amber Novak, you're home, I told myself sternly. *You're beginning a new phase of your life. Just like Hazel says, you've got to make the best of what you've got.*

9

~~~

As Jack predicted, my discharge from Hamilton was timed for my return to school. I had just a week to get used to my new life at home before classes began. I noticed that Mom spent a lot of time on the phone, making arrangements with Mr. Hartman. I was the first wheelchair-using student they'd ever had at Central High, and everyone seemed to be in a tizzy.

On the opening day of the fall semester, I was ready with my new pens, folders, and bundle of notebooks. My brand-new backpack hung behind me on the back of my wheelchair.

If only Jack were beside me now, I thought, as Mom pulled my chair from the backseat and unfolded it in the school parking lot. If only my friends from D-4 were gathered around me, so I wouldn't be the only kid in a wheelchair this morning! But I was alone—no, it was worse than alone. My mother was with me. She hadn't merely driven me to school. She had come today on a mission—to make sure I got safely into the building, to be certain I reached my homeroom, to talk to my teachers, to make arrangements as needed. Last spring I couldn't have imagined starting a new school year with my mom in tow. Now, in this new life, I seemed to have no choice.

Mom bent and checked the brake on my chair. I waited for her to help me transfer, the way Dad always did when he was around. But Mom waited, too, looking at me expectantly. "Come on," she said. "You don't want to be late your first morning."

"I don't want to land on the pavement my first morning, either," I grumbled. If she was so determined to do something for me, she could at least help where it mattered.

Mom didn't reply. She was ready to out-wait me. I slid to the edge of the car seat and planted my right hand on the seat of the wheelchair. Fueled by my anger, I swung my body across the yawning distance. I plopped down so hard I felt the jolt through the back of my head. But I had done it, with no help from anyone. *Carlos would be proud of me*, I thought. In fact, I was proud of myself.

Fortunately, Mom had agreed that we come early, well ahead of the crowd. The parking lot was nearly empty, and none of my fellow students were in sight as I wheeled around to the side entrance. According to Mr. Hartman, it would be the easiest one for me to use, with only two steps leading up to it. The other entrances all had four steps, and one even had six.

Mr. Hartman himself was there to welcome us, with Mrs. Gambino standing faithfully by his side. Mom greeted them effusively, as if they were all old friends. She had spent hours on the phone with them, and had even visited the school to measure doorways and bathroom stalls.

"Hello, young lady," Mr. Hartman said, stooping to pat my shoulder. "Ready for vacation to be over?"

What vacation was he talking about? What did he think I'd been doing all summer—playing tennis? Suddenly I remembered the last time he and I had met, when he had roared, "This is a high school, not a dance club!" Back then I'd believed that wearing an ugly granny sweater was the worst thing that could possibly happen to me!

I put my hand over my mouth to suppress a giggle. "What's so amusing, young lady?" Mr. Hartman inquired.

"Nothing," I said. He didn't seem to remember I was the dress-code delinquent, the girl who had worn that treacherous shirt that left an inch of midriff exposed.

"She looks all bright-eyed and bushy-tailed, doesn't she?" Mrs. Gambino said above my head. I was sure she didn't remember me either. She didn't remember leading me and Katrina through the labyrinth behind the main office, and extracting The Sweater from that musty drawer. I was an entirely different person to them now. I wasn't a girl who tested the rules, but a kid in a wheelchair who somehow had to be hoisted up two daunting cement steps.

Mr. Hartman turned back to Mom. "I called a couple of the kids in our Key Club," he explained. "Big strong guys who might not mind helping out. We'll have it set up by the end of the week. I can get her up myself in the meantime, or get a custodian to help." He bent to seize my chair by the footrest. I grabbed the armrests for dear life.

"It works best if—" Mom began. She stopped herself and turned to me. "Amber, you explain it. You know better than anybody else."

How was I supposed to tell Mr. Hartman what to do? He was the principal. He was the one who gave the orders around here. But Mom was right. On this one, I knew more than the principal did. "Take hold of the handles in back," I said. "You can pull the chair up backwards, it's easier."

"Hold tight, young lady!" Mr. Hartman said jovially. He seized the handles and hauled me up to the landing with two mighty bumps.

"It'll be a lot more fun with some nice, strong boys to help you," Mrs. Gambino promised. Her knowing little laugh made me shudder.

With one more bump Mr. Hartman lifted me over the door sill. I was inside at last, on the level linoleum of the first floor. Mr. Hartman handed me my class schedule. My eyes ran down the list: First Period—Algebra Two, Room 114; Second Period—Chorale, Room 103; Third Period—Computer Science, Room 131 . . .

"I didn't sign up for computers!" I protested. "I'm supposed to have biology."

Mr. Hartman didn't answer directly. "All her classes meet on this floor," he explained to Mom. "We had to do some juggling, but Mrs. Gambino and I worked it out."

"What about biology?" I asked again, in case he hadn't heard me.

"Yes, well . . . " Mr. Hartman cleared his throat. "We had to make a few adjustments."

Mrs. Gambino tried to help him out. "You know the biology lab is upstairs," she told me with a sugary smile. "We had to choose something else for you. If you're not happy with the computer course, we'll have to make another change, I suppose."

"But I'm a junior. I've got to take science this year. I need the credits so I can graduate." It was one thing to tell the principal how to lift me up steps. But why did I have to explain to him about my course requirements? It didn't make sense!

"What about the elevator?" Mom asked. "You said Amber might be able to use it."

Mr. Hartman cleared his throat again. "I've explained this to you, Mrs. Novak. It's a freight elevator. Only the custodians are allowed to have the keys."

Mom looked distressed. "You were going to work something out," she said. "You said you'd try to get Amber her own elevator key."

"It's not as easy as you think," Mr. Hartman said. "I'm not free to make that decision myself.

It would have to go through channels, and that takes time. Meanwhile, Amber needs to get started taking whatever classes she can."

"What about lunch?" I asked. "How will I get downstairs to the cafeteria?"

"For the time being, one of the custodians will take you down," Mr. Hartman said. "He'll meet you by the elevator during your lunch period."

I studied my schedule again. Even my homeroom had been shifted. I should have been in 214, on the second floor, with the other juniors whose last names began with N. Now I was reassigned to 122. "It's still a junior homeroom," Mrs. Gambino insisted. "You'll be with the Gs this year. You don't mind, do you?"

"I've got nothing against the Gs," I said. "But I had friends in my old room. I'll miss them."

The 8:10 bell rang. Not many people used the side entrance, and the hall was still quiet. But kids were starting to trickle in. They came in twos and threes, heads bent together, voices filled with laughter and excitement. Boys pushed each other good-naturedly, while girls talked at high speed. Some of the kids were so busy they didn't glance our way. Some looked in our direction and picked up their pace to get past us. Some came to a full stop, and I felt their stares drill straight into me. It was as though I were some strange creature they wanted to dissect before the opening assembly.

"Can I go to my locker now?" I asked. "It's getting to be time."

"Go ahead," Mom said. "I want to talk with Mr. Hartman a few more minutes. I'll see you at three o'clock."

"Okay," I said. As I started down the hall, I turned and added, "Thanks for the ride—and everything."

Naturally, I had a new locker next to my new homeroom, and naturally, the combination didn't work. From my sitting position I could barely reach the dial. I studied the slip with the instructions and tried again. Right to 39, left to 17, right to 28 . . . I jiggled the handle, but the door still refused to budge.

"Amber! There you are! They stuck you way down here?" Katrina loped toward me, fresh and polished, ready to start the new year. I felt battered and woebegone beside her.

"I've got to have all my classes on the first floor," I explained. "And now I can't open my locker. I feel like a stupid freshman!"

Katrina glanced at the combination slip and tried her hand with the dial. After the fourth attempt she kicked at the metal door in frustration.

"It's all right," I said. "I'll worry about it later."

A knot of kids tightened around us. I tried to believe that they hadn't stopped to look at me in my wheelchair. *It was always possible*, I told myself, *that they had a consuming interest in jammed lockers*.

"Get the custodian," one girl suggested.

"Or a crowbar," a boy said helpfully.

"Hey, just ram it with your chair!" another boy said. He gestured with his hands and made a sound like shellfire.

"Amber, may I give it a try?"

It was a boy's voice—familiar, careful, questioning. It struck me to the heart. For a long moment I couldn't move, couldn't even think. At last I turned my head enough to confirm what I knew already. Eric Moore stood at the edge of the crowd. Our eyes met in a swift, frightened glance.

"Can I try?" he repeated. "Sometimes I'm good at combinations."

"Sure," I said. I moved aside and gave him

the combination slip. Eric spun the dial so fast he didn't seem to stop at the proper numbers. He waited half a second, then lifted the handle. The door swung open.

"Thank you," I said stiffly. "I don't know how you did it."

"Me, neither," he said. "I got lucky this time."

My heart pounded frantically. How could I sit here talking to Eric about locker combinations? I had to say something else. He had to say something else to me.

"Aw, man!" said the shellfire boy. "That was no fun!"

"Sorry about that," said Eric. The 8:25 bell rang. In four minutes more we should all be seated in our homerooms. I was no longer the center of attention.

"See you, Amber," Eric said as the crowd dispersed.

"Bye," I said. I don't know if he heard me as he headed for the stairs.

"Was that weird or what?" Katrina asked as Eric disappeared.

"It was weird," I said. "I don't want to talk about it."

"He was trying to be nice," she said.

"So was I. And I don't want to talk about it any more."

My hands shook as I sorted through my backpack. I stashed a load of supplies in my locker and banged the door shut. How would I open it when I needed to get into it again? How would I stop my hands from trembling each time I caught a glimpse of Eric Moore?

10

—⁓—

Usually not much studying happens on the first day of a new school year. Most teachers use the time to hand out books and lay down the law. Mine tried to outdo one another on that opening day, warning us how strict they intended to be and how challenging they would make their assignments. They tried to win us over by throwing in a few jokes, but that didn't change the message underneath. Summer was over. It was time to get down to serious business.

I didn't get much information about computers or algebra that first day back at school, but I learned a lot of other things I had never known before. I learned that only one girls' bathroom on the entire first floor had a toilet stall big enough for a wheelchair to enter. I

learned that there was a series of four steps
between the back of the auditorium and the
front, so during Chorale I had to sit in the back
row. I learned that custodians are very busy people, and when they promise to meet you by the
elevator at lunchtime, they're likely to forget.
How had I lived without suspecting these things
before? They were so crucial now, so absolutely
central to my life.

I learned other lessons, too, that were even
harder to absorb. Coming back to my old crowd
of friends was more difficult than I could have
imagined. The awkwardness of Katrina's first
visit to the hospital seemed to play over and
over as I moved through the day. People I'd
known since junior high went tongue-tied in my
presence. They looked up and down, right and
left, desperate to get away. When I asked Maura
Shehan about her summer, I had to drag the stories out in broken fragments. She never asked
me about my summer in return. I got the distinct
feeling that she was afraid to hear the details.
When I told Cori Madison I liked the decals on
her locker, she answered that I was the bravest
person she'd ever met.

She was trying to compliment me, but somehow her words didn't feel like praise. "What are

you talking about?" I demanded. "I haven't done anything brave."

"Well, you're here," Cori said, flustered. "I mean, that took a lot of courage, didn't it?"

"You're here too," I countered. "Was it brave of you to come to school this morning?"

"It's different," she protested. "For me it's the same as it always was. But for you . . . " She blushed furiously. She couldn't say the words that blazed between us.

I had to rescue her. "We're all brave for coming in today," I said, trying to laugh. "Did you take a look at that syllabus for American lit? It's twelve pages long!"

"Not a pretty sight," Cori agreed. But she wasn't ready to let go of the courage topic. "The thing is," she said, "you have to do all the regular things like the rest of us—only you have this extra hard part attached."

Everything Cori said made sense. Yet somehow it didn't feel right to me. I struggled to sort it out for both of us. "I think courage is when you've got a choice," I said at last. "Like suppose you see a house on fire. You can stay outside where it's safe, or choose to go in and save the kids. I didn't choose anything. I just came to school."

"I might've stayed home if I were you," Cori said.

"You'd get bored," I told her. "I sure do, sitting around all day."

That wasn't quite right either, I realized. I took one final stab. "I want to be out, doing things," I said. "The same things I used to do. The same as always."

I'm not sure Cori understood, but talking with her helped clarify something in my own mind. My first day back at school confronted me with countless inconveniences, even humiliations. But I felt alive in a way that I hadn't since the accident. I was out in the world again. I was among friends and strangers, and for better or for worse, I was making my own way. This was where I truly belonged.

"How did it go today?" Dad asked at dinner.

"Okay," I said. He wouldn't want to know about the bathrooms, the auditorium, and the awkward, curious stares. He still studied the Internet night after night, looking for phantom cures. I didn't want to remind him about the hard parts of my new lifestyle—it would make him feel all the more desperate.

"That principal over there is a typical

bureaucrat," Mom said, reaching for the basket of rolls. "You can't get a straight answer out of him."

"I thought you guys were so buddy-buddy!" I said, amazed.

"It's all a game," Mom said. "I try to butter him up so he'll give us what we need. He tries to sweet-talk me so I'll go along with him when he says no."

I looked at my mother with new admiration. "At school everybody calls him Heartless," I said. "Not just on account of his name, either."

"I had no idea there would be so many roadblocks," Mom said. "This isn't supposed to happen, according to the law."

"You mean that disability law?" I asked. "Aaron told me something about it once."

"The ADA, the Americans with Disabilities Act," Mom said. "Schools, public buildings, offices—they're supposed to make reasonable accommodations so everybody can use them."

"What's reasonable?" asked Max through a mouthful.

"That's the big question," Mom sighed. "Nothing is, according to this Hartman character. We ask for the simplest things, and he acts like we're demanding half his salary."

"I had to eat in the office today," I said. "When can I get my own key to the elevator?"

"When?" Mom repeated. "This guy doesn't answer questions like 'When?' All you get out of him is double-talk."

Max put down his fork and stared. "Amber!" he exclaimed. "You mean there's an elevator right there, and they won't let you use it?"

Dad spoke for the first time. "It's a freight elevator. It isn't designed for passengers. They told us it's a safety issue."

"But people must ride in it sometimes," Max insisted. "The freight doesn't go up and down all by itself."

We all looked at Dad, waiting for his response. He sawed at his meat, thinking. "They really should let you use the elevator at least," he said at last. "It isn't like you're asking them to build ramps and all that."

"But I wish they would!" I burst out. "I don't want to be carried in and out of the building every day! It's awful."

"It won't be forever," Dad said. "Just till you get back on your feet."

There it was again—Dad's hope, Dad's promise. His words had an unreal quality now, like Cori's talk about bravery. No doctor on earth had the power to mend my broken spinal cord. I couldn't spend the rest of my life waiting for a miracle. We needed to focus on more immediate things—like a way for me to get in and out of the school building independently.

No one had homework that night, so when Katrina dropped in after supper, we had time for a long visit. She arrived bursting with news.

"What's up?" I asked when we got settled in my room.

"You know how we wanted to start a band last spring?" she asked. "We used to talk about it all the time, remember?"

My mind reached back to that long-ago time before the accident. "Sure," I said. "I've hardly thought about it in months."

"Well, I have!" Katrina said triumphantly. "Me on keyboard, you as lead singer. We just needed a drummer and a guitar."

"Oh, that's all?" I said, laughing. "How about amplifiers and microphones and—and practice! And somebody who wants to listen to us!"

"Come on," she pleaded. "You don't have to think that far ahead!"

"Okay, so we need a drummer and a bass player. I'll go along with that."

"Good," she said. "Because we've got them!"

"Who?" I demanded. "Where did you find them?"

"The drummer's a guy named Pete who just moved in down the street from me. He's really cute, too, wait till you see him!"

"And who's the bass player?" I pressed.

"You know Michael Framer? He's kind of short, red hair."

"His name's familiar. I think I've seen him."

"Well, Pete knows him real well. Pete asked him if he'd join up with us, and he said yes. So we're all set!"

"We are?" Her enthusiasm was catching, but I didn't want to get carried away.

"My parents will let us practice in the basement," Katrina said. I opened my mouth to ask how I would get down the stairs, but she hurried on, "We've got an attached garage, remember? You can go in that way, and it's perfectly level."

It was as though a door swung open in my imagination, revealing a dazzling array of possibilities. Rehearsals, agents, live performances on MTV—I vaulted from my humdrum existence to a world of glamor. Cameras flashed, crowds cheered, my hand ached from signing my autograph, and the limo was waiting. . . .

"So, Saturday at ten o'clock," Katrina said.

"We'll break for lunch and work some more in the afternoon."

The limo vanished, and the crowd melted away. "This is for real," I said. "You're not just talking about it."

"Since when do I just talk about things?" Katrina asked. "I'm a mover and a shaker!"

"We have a name!" I remembered suddenly. "Legacy."

"That's great," Katrina said. "Especially if we do some eighties stuff. Where'd you come up with that?"

The name floated before me, disembodied. I had no idea where it came from. And then I remembered. I sat beside Eric in history class, bundled in my granny sweater.

"I didn't think it up myself," I admitted. "It came from Eric Moore."

II

~~~

"One more time!" Katrina called. "Take it from the top!"

Katrina led with the opener on the keyboard. Pete came in, accenting the rhythm with his drums. Michael's first notes on the guitar signaled my entrance. I opened my mouth and began to sing. Amplified by the microphone, my voice seemed to fill the basement rec room. It resounded from the walls and ceiling, bigger than me, bigger than life.

"This is going to work!" Katrina said gleefully when we got to the end. "That was great, Amber! Your voice has a terrific range."

"The Beatles started in a basement, too, did you know that?" Pete asked. "Let's do a couple Beatles tunes."

"Oh, come on," Katrina protested. "I thought Legacy was about eighties music. We're not playing nursing homes, are we?"

"We might get a job at a wedding," I pointed out. "All the generations at one party."

"We've got to have the standards down," Pete persisted. "You know, like 'Michelle.' And 'Yesterday.'"

Katrina made a face, but she struck up the opening chords. I didn't need sheet music. Some songs you just pick up unconsciously, through a lifetime of exposure. "Yesterday," I began soulfully, "All my troubles seemed so far away . . . "

I'd heard that old song a thousand times, but I never thought about the words before. Now the song spoke to me as if it were brand-new. What troubles did I have in all my yesterdays before the accident? Of course I worried about things back then, and had bad days as well as good ones. But all those problems seemed trivial as I looked back. I never appreciated the easy, normal life I had until it was snatched away from me. As I sang the song's last refrain, my eyes welled with tears. "Oh, I believe in yesterday . . . "

When Katrina strummed the last mournful chord, the boys burst into applause. "You were really getting into it, Amber," Pete exclaimed. "You'll give a three-hanky performance!"

Michael nodded. He fit the definition of the strong, silent type. We'd been practicing for two hours already and I hadn't yet heard him utter a complete sentence.

Katrina was in charge, and she was not one to let us relax and enjoy our accomplishments. "One more, and then we'll take a food break," she announced. "I made a bunch of sandwiches. We can eat down here."

Katrina might be the leader, but she didn't have total control. Pete declared we should work on something by Greenday, and Katrina wanted a Meatloaf number. Michael waited patiently, tuning his bass. My thoughts drifted away from the debate. Whatever we played was fine with me. I was happy just being here, with a group of kids, doing something we all enjoyed and cared about.

Just as Katrina promised, practicing at her house was virtually problem-free. There were no steps between the garage and the basement, only a threshold so low I could roll up and over without help. Once inside, I found a wide, uncluttered room where I had complete freedom of movement. There was an awkward moment when Pete set up the mike stand, only to discover it was impossibly high for anyone in a seated position. Katrina told me not to worry, and found a microphone that clipped onto my collar. "This kind is better anyway," she said. "You don't get all those screeches and echoes." She wasn't saying that to make me feel better. It was actually true.

"Okay, let's do Greenday," Katrina decided. "Just mouth the words if you don't know them, Amber."

"I can lip sync," I said. "Whatever."

Katrina made a halting start, broke off, and began again. The drums were off this time, the bass got lost, and before I had a chance to show how many words I didn't remember, Katrina called a halt. "Wow!" she said. "That was a mess!"

"We'll work on it," I said. "That's what practices are for."

"Over and over and over!" Michael said. He didn't need a full sentence to get the point across. We'd go back again and again until we got it right. We were in this together, as equals. Combining our talents, the four of us were Legacy.

• • •

"Heave ho! Up you go!" Ryan Gray said cheerfully. I leaned back as he pulled my chair up the steps to the side entrance. Ryan was good. This was his third morning in a row to help me, and by now he had the system down. I liked his manner, the easy way he joked with me. He acted as though helping me up the steps was no big deal—an ordinary favor he might do for any ordinary person.

Even so, I hated the process of getting in and out of the school building each day. Sometimes I sat for ten minutes at the foot of the steps, waiting for whichever of the Key Club boys was assigned to help me. I felt horribly conspicuous as other kids filed past me. Some rushed by without a glance. Some paused to smile and say hello before they hurried away. Everyone had places to go and schedules to keep. I was left behind, to wait.

When Katrina was around, she stayed to keep me company. We always had plenty to talk about, and the time flew by. I knew she wanted to be with me, that she enjoyed those extra minutes together before classes began. But I also knew she needed to get inside, to stop at her locker, to run errands before homeroom. It was bad enough that I had to be late. If Katrina hung around with me, she ended up being late, too.

Why couldn't school be like practices in Katrina's basement, I asked myself as I headed down the hall. By now, three weeks into the term, people were more used to seeing me in my wheelchair, and I didn't draw so many curious stares. But I was always aware that I was missing out on things because so much of the building was inaccessible. Beyond the first floor, everything was off-limits. Yet Mr. Hartman—Heartless—still refused to give me a key to the freight elevator. I was only allowed to use it if one of the custodians accompanied me. Since the custodians were usually mopping floors and scrubbing bathrooms, they were seldom around when I needed them. I still spent most lunch periods in the main office, with Mrs. Gambino fluttering around me like a mother hen.

For the past three weeks Mr. Hartman had hedged and stalled. The freight elevator was unsafe, he insisted. There was a question of insurance. Besides, my use of the elevator would set a bad precedent for the other students. If I were allowed to use it, my classmates would expect the same privilege. Others would start riding up and down along with me. Some unprincipled opportunist might even get hold of the key and make copies. Pretty soon the whole situation would be completely out of hand. Mr. Hartman would have to look into it further. There was a great deal to consider.

When I was in the hospital, Mom reminded me to co-operate, to do whatever the staff told me to do. Now, dealing with Mr. Hartman, everything was different. Co-operation was getting us nowhere. Finally Mom decided to bypass Mr. Hartman altogether. She took the question of the freight elevator directly to the school board. She made phone calls and wrote letters. This morning, at the end of second period, Mom and I were scheduled to meet with Mr. Hartman to hear the board's final decision.

My morning classes dragged by. Time moved so slowly, the clock seemed to be running backwards. Surely the board would be reasonable! Surely they would want me to have access to the whole building with all of my classmates. How could they possibly say no to such a simple request? But then I thought of Mr. Hartman. He'd been saying no for weeks now, in his vague, indecisive way. Maybe the board was composed of people who thought the same way he did.

It was hard to maneuver through the crowds in the halls, so I was allowed to leave my classes three minutes before the bell rang. Since I sat in the back of the auditorium during Chorale, I slipped out easily without attracting much notice. In the empty corridor I went into high speed. My chair zoomed to the end of the hall, whipped around the corner, and made a straight shot for the Main Office. Mom waited for me at the door.

"What do you think?" I asked her. "Are they going to say yes?"

"I wish they would have let us attend the meeting," Mom sighed. "Why should a school board be allowed to hold closed meetings, anyway?"

"So they can say whatever they want and it won't get back to us," I said.

Mrs. Gambino fluttered to greet us when we entered the office. "Mr. Hartman will be right with you," she said, herding us to his inner chamber. "Can I get you coffee? No? A cup of tea maybe? One of the secretaries brought in some nice coffee. . . . "

Mom finally accepted a cup of coffee, just to calm Mrs. Gambino down. I sat with my hands on my lap, gazing at the framed photograph on the opposite wall. It showed Mr. Hartman with his wife and a boy of four or five who had to be their son. They all stood stiffly, smiling for the camera. I couldn't guess what any of them was thinking.

As Mom and I sat in Mr. Hartman's office I had a revelation of truth. People don't keep you waiting when they have good news to share. Mr. Hartman arrived a full fifteen minutes late.

He breezed in with a vague apology—something about one of the schoolbuses being late. For a long minute he fiddled with a bunch of papers on his desk. At last Mom broke the silence. "I understand that the school board met last night."

"Yes. Yes, the board did meet," Mr. Hartman said. "And your daughter's—Amber's—situation was discussed."

"What did they say?" I asked. "Can I finally have my own key to the elevator?"

Mr. Hartman's smile looked as if it were pasted onto his face. "Hold on, young lady," he said. "Let me explain a few things."

"I don't know what you need to explain," Mom said. Her voice was calm, but I knew she was boiling inside. "Amber asked a direct question. Is the answer yes or is it no?"

"Just hear me out, Mrs. Novak!" Mr. Hartman protested. "Give me a few moments, please."

"What did the school board decide?" Mom repeated. "Tell us."

Mr. Hartman tilted back in his chair. He cleared his throat, and we waited.

"You need to understand," he began at last, "that the school board has never faced a—a situation like this before. This is the first time our school has been asked to accommodate someone who—" He looked at me briefly and turned back to Mom. "Someone in your daughter's—circumstances."

He paused to let his words sink in. When neither of us spoke, he went on. "The board is very concerned that Amber receive the best possible education. The members of the board would like to see her as happy and as comfortable as she can be."

He cleared his throat again. "Do you follow me so far?" he asked, as though he had just put a set of equations on the blackboard.

I nodded obediently, but Mom looked blank. "What did they say about the elevator?" she asked again.

"The elevator is only the beginning," Mr. Hartman said. "Even if Amber were to use the elevator any time she chooses, there would still be problems. There are steps in the auditorium, as you know. There is only one girls' bathroom she can use. Not one of our drinking fountains is low enough for someone in her situation to reach. And, of course, there are steps at all of our entrances."

"Yes, there are a lot of adaptations that still need to be made," Mom said. "But the elevator will make a huge difference. She'll have free access to all of the classrooms."

Mr. Hartman held up his hand for silence. "The board would love to make every adaptation that Amber needs. But it just isn't feasible. There's the cost factor. The school has to operate within its budget."

"But it won't cost anything for me to use the elevator," I pointed out. "It doesn't cost much to get a key copied."

He shot me a frown. Clearly I had spoken out of turn. "Now, over in Naperville there is a high school that's fully adapted for students with—with all kinds of handicaps. It's called Open Door. If Amber transfers there, she'll have everything she needs. It will be the perfect environment for her."

"Wait a second!" I exclaimed. "I don't want to transfer!"

"I think you'd be a lot happier in the long

run," he said with another pasted-on smile. "You wouldn't feel so alone."

"Who says I feel alone now?" I cried. "I have friends here. Kids I've known since seventh grade!"

"But here you're the only one who's—" he seemed at a loss, but finally managed to croak out the words, "confined to a wheelchair."

"We put a question to the board about the elevator," Mom said. "What is the board's answer to that question?"

"The board recommends a transfer," Mr. Hartman said. "It recommends that your daughter transfer to Open Door High School as soon as possible."

12

~~~

I didn't shed a tear in Mr. Hartman's office. I refused to let him see my frustration, my hurt, my helpless rage. I didn't even cry in front of Mom when we got back out to the hall again. She had fought for me with all her strength, and we had lost. I needed to give her my support and my appreciation. It was no time for me to collapse into despair.

"We'll have to go over to Open Door and take a look," Mom said wearily. "If it's really awful, we can use that as another argument."

I pictured a school building with all its doors flung wide, as stray dogs, pigeons, and winter gales rushed in. "What kind of name is Open Door?" I asked, trying to laugh. "Sounds like it'd be freezing in January."

Mom didn't even crack a smile. "I'll make an appointment," she said. "We'll go one day this week and see what the place is about."

I didn't cry until the beginning of lunch period, as I waited vainly by the locked freight elevator for a custodian who failed to appear. Everyone else thundered downstairs until at last the corridor was empty. I sat alone, left behind. The endless question circled through my brain: why wouldn't they simply give me a key? It would be such an easy gesture, and it would mean so much in my life! How could they say no?

Then, for the second time that morning, I had a revelation. With a jarring bolt of certainty, I realized that the elevator key was not the real issue. Mr. Hartman said so himself this morning in his office. Even if they gave me the key, there were still the steps, the fountains, the bathroom stalls, the unreachably tall bookcases in the library. The school was a minefield of obstacles. Everywhere I turned, I was reminded that I was different because I used a wheelchair.

If they gave me a key to the elevator, surely we would make other requests. Then there was that safety question I heard again and again. If Ryan or one of the other Key Club boys lost his hold, if I tumbled down the steps and got hurt, would my family start a lawsuit? Maybe the real issue was money. Mr. Hartman was a typical bureaucrat, as Mom pointed out. His mission in life was to keep expenses down.

Yet money was only part of the story. Something even deeper was going on. Why did Mr. Hartman always refer to my "situation" and my "circumstances"? Why was it so hard for him to say the word "wheelchair?" He was just as uncomfortable with my disability as the kids who shied away from me in the halls. No wonder he wanted me to transfer to another school! If I went to Open Door, he wouldn't have to think any more about me and my problems. He wouldn't have to see me every day and wonder how he should handle my "situation." He could congratulate himself for sending me to a place that was safe and accessible, a place specially designed for people like me.

Wasn't it bad enough that I'd been injured in the accident? Wasn't learning to use a wheelchair enough of a challenge? I had worked so hard all those months at Hamilton. I had learned everything I could in order to meet the world again. I wanted to resume my old life with my old friends. And now, after everything I'd

been through, Mr. Hartman and the school
board told me I was no longer welcome at Central High. I belonged someplace else. I had to
live among other people, people who were as
different and unwelcome as I was myself.

I couldn't walk anymore, but I was the person I'd always been. Didn't anybody see me?
When they looked at me, did people see Amber
Novak, the aspiring singer, Amber, who wore
dangly earrings and bangle bracelets? Or did
they see only my wheelchair, as though I wasn't
here at all?

Sometimes when you cry, you hope someone
will come along to comfort you. You want to
pour your troubles into a sympathetic ear, to
hear a kind voice promise that everything will
be all right. But when I began to cry that morning, sitting in the hall by the freight elevator, I
was glad that I was alone. I didn't want anyone
to see me like this, shaking with sobs, helpless
with despair. No one could ease this hurt with
mere words. No human touch could take this
misery away.

Suddenly a hollow, disembodied voice broke
through to me. "Attention, all students and faculty," Mr. Hartman boomed from a speaker on
the wall. "I want to remind all of you that there

will be a pep rally this afternoon at 2:30. At the end of seventh period, we will all gather on the athletic field."

He sounded so brisk and efficient, conducting business as usual. What would he say if he saw me here, crying myself inside out? Probably he'd say it made perfect sense. Life in a wheelchair was a burden to me, no wonder I was falling to pieces. It just proved that he was right, and I couldn't function in a standard environment with normal people.

Suddenly a wave of anger overcame my tears. The Mr. Hartmans of the world wouldn't beat me down! I would never let them sweep me aside. They wouldn't see me cry! They wouldn't see me be defeated!

I rummaged in my backpack and pulled out a handful of Kleenex. After I blew my nose and wiped my eyes, I got out my makeup kit and tried to compose myself. My face still looked a little puffy by the time I finished, but I didn't think anyone would notice unless they looked carefully.

My lunch was in my backpack, too. Obviously I couldn't eat in the cafeteria today. I would have to sit in the office again, with Mrs. Gambino buzzing around me like a pesky fly. I would have to sit there again like a convict, awaiting my sentence.

Drearily I headed down the hall, back to the Main Office. I felt as though I spent half my life there! It wasn't fair! I hadn't cut class or talked back to a teacher or pilfered anyone's lunch money. I hadn't even violated the dress code! My only crime was using a wheelchair. I was being sent to the office because I couldn't walk up and down stairs.

I stopped abruptly and made a U-turn in the middle of the corridor. I'd find somewhere else to go, I resolved. I'd find somewhere pleasant and quiet where I could eat by myself, safe from pitying stares.

I wheeled past the gym, past the guidance office and the art rooms. The corridor branched into a short hallway, the music wing. Someone was practicing a clarinet, the notes warm and comforting through the closed door of the band room. I could sit here, undisturbed, and listen. I would be in good company, the company of that unseen musician playing little runs and ripples of notes.

But I wasn't alone. A figure hunched on the window ledge at the end of the hall. It was a boy with thick, sandy hair, his head down, his face half hidden. He looked as if he were trying to become invisible—yet he was utterly familiar.

I would recognize him anywhere. It was Eric Moore.

I was certain he hadn't seen me. He didn't lift his head. He didn't move at all, just huddled there alone at the window. Silently I backed away, turned, and sped around the corner. I didn't stop till I reached the thick rubber mat by the front door. My heart was racing, and my hands shook.

Was this the Eric Moore I remembered— always laughing, always jostling ahead, never wasting time, never looking back? Was this Eric the linebacker, Eric the life of the party? What was he doing in the music wing where no one would think to look for him, alone with the wistful notes of a clarinet drifting around him?

Maybe I should go back, I thought wildly. *Maybe I should try to speak to him.* But he had chosen that spot, a place where no one would ever think to look for him. Surely he wanted to be by himself. It was a feeling I understood.

I forgot all about eating lunch. I even forgot about Mr. Hartman and Open Door High School. The picture of Eric, hunched on the window ledge, filled my whole mind. I remembered what

Katrina said last spring when she visited me at Hamilton, that Eric walked around school like a zombie. Back then I'd thought it was only fair that he should suffer. I was miserable and I wanted him to be miserable, too. Now I had caught a glimpse of Eric in pain, and it tore at my heart.

Maybe he'd had a fight with his parents. Maybe the coach just told him he'd have to warm the bench at Saturday's game. Maybe his unhappiness had nothing to do with the accident last spring.

But he'd sent that pleading note. He said there were things he wanted to tell me. Again and again I had refused to hear him.

I didn't know what drove Eric to that lonesome corner today. But somehow I would have to find out.

13

~~~

On Friday Mom drove me over to Naperville to visit Open Door High School. "Its doors may be open," I quipped as we crossed the parking lot, "but my mind sure isn't."

"Try to give it a chance," Mom pleaded. She looked exhausted. She had given up the fight with Mr. Hartman. She hoped I would accept the transfer and adjust happily to my new school. There would be an end to negotiations with bureaucrats, an end to questions of how much or how little to request. But I would never accept being pushed aside, I thought fiercely. I would never adjust to a second-rate life.

"Which entrance do I have to use?" I asked as we neared the building. "Are we supposed to go around to the side?"

"No," Mom said. "When I talked to the principal, she said any door's okay. They have ramps at all of them."

"All of them?" I repeated skeptically.

"That's what she said," Mom insisted. "We'll see."

As I expected, half a dozen daunting steps led up to the main entrance. But to my amazement, a graceful ramp curved beside them, all the way to the front door. I leaned back in my chair and glided up, wholly under my own power. As I approached the door, it whished open, just like the magic doors back at Hamilton Hospital. "Pretty neat!" I exclaimed. "No wonder it's called Open Door!"

Mom and I headed down the wide, bright corridor to the office. "Look!" I said as we passed a drinking fountain. "I could reach that! It's just the right height!"

At the office Mom went to one of the secretaries—Ms. Galloway, according to the sign over her desk. "We're here to meet with the principal," she explained. "Mrs. Sanchez."

"Oh, you must be the Novaks," the secretary said. "Hold on, I'll let her know you're here." She spoke quickly into the phone and turned back to us. "She'll be right with you," she said. "Three or four minutes."

As we waited, a tall, skinny boy rushed in behind us. He hurried to Ms. Galloway's desk and launched into a series of frantic gestures, his face a picture of distress. To my amazement, Ms. Galloway responded with the same silent hand signals. They were using sign language, I realized in wonder. Was the boy deaf? Ms. Galloway could hear—she talked to us and spoke on the telephone. How did she know sign language?

I had no idea what she told him, but her signs had a calming effect. Ms. Galloway picked up the phone again, and I heard her explaining, "Mrs. Malony? Brandon's here, and he wants to try out for varsity basketball this afternoon. He says he forgot his permission slip. He needs you to come in and sign—"

I didn't hear the rest. A door whished open, and from the inner office came a small, smiling woman with her gray hair in a twisted braid. She wore purple slacks and a matching jacket. And she came toward us in a gleaming red wheelchair!

"Hi," she said, her voice sparkling. "Amber Novak, I presume?"

Since the accident I'd been subjected to every possible variation on the human stare, from wide-eyed amazement to bold curiosity and open-mouthed shock. I knew from the inside how awful it felt to be stared at. Yet here I was, staring at Mrs. Sanchez in her sleek red chair. My eyes swept up and down, from her face to the chair and back to her face again, trying to take in what I was seeing.

Mom was the first to speak. "Hello," she said, and her voice told me that she was startled, too. "It's so nice to meet you, after talking the other day."

This woman couldn't be the principal, I thought wildly. Probably she was here to help the disabled students. The real principal, the person truly in charge, had to be someone else.

Mrs. Sanchez brought her chair beside mine so she could offer me her hand. It was as warm and welcoming as her smile. "You look a little surprised," she said. "You didn't expect me to be a wheelchair-user, did you?"

"No," I gasped. "I never thought about it."

"Never thought that a school principal could use a wheelchair?"

"No," I said honestly. "But you're not the *real* principal, are you?"

"I was last time I looked," she said.

"I mean," I faltered, "you're just the principal for the disabled students, right? Not for everybody."

"We don't make those distinctions around here," she assured me. "We're all in it together."

"But you have a special program," Mom said. "You have all these special services."

"The whole school benefits," Mrs. Sanchez explained patiently. "Okay, for kids who can't use stairs, we put in elevators. But everybody can use them, now that they're here. It's great when you've got forty pounds of books in your backpack."

"No keys!" I marveled. "No arguments!"

"When they hired me ten years ago, this school was pretty typical," she went on. "No one had ever thought about how to include students with disabilities. We didn't have many, and the ones we did have were left out of a lot."

"You mean they hired you to be in charge of a regular school?" I exclaimed. "Not a special school for wheelchair kids?"

"We've always been a regular school," Mrs. Sanchez said. "But over the years we've worked to make the whole program accessible to everybody. We put in a couple of elevators. We started teaching American Sign Language to the students and staff. We've got computers with speech output for kids who can't see the screen."

"It sounds so basic," Mom sighed. "At Central we're fighting every inch of the way."

"I keep hoping we'll be a model for other schools," Mrs. Sanchez said. "I've got to admit, I cringed when the board asked to change our name to Open Door. It sounds so syrupy. But I guess it's a small price to pay, they've been so co-operative about everything else."

"Can you show us around?" I asked. I was startled by the eagerness in my own voice.

"We're on the same page," Mrs. Sanchez said. "Let's check out the chemistry lab first, it's right around the corner."

"Wait," Ms. Galloway called. "You've got four messages. One from Maintenance about the windows in the East Wing. One about that administrators' conference, and—"

"As soon as I get back," Mrs. Sanchez said. "These folks have been patient."

I loved the way Ms. Galloway spoke to her, with respect and a touch of exasperation. Mrs. Sanchez was busy, with people lining up to talk to her. She was an important person, red wheelchair and all.

Mom trailed behind as Mrs. Sanchez and I sped down the corridor. In the chemistry lab, everything was at easy wheelchair height—the tables, the racks of test tubes, the counters and sinks. All of the kids in the room were stilt-walkers, as Aaron would have called them. "How many wheelchair kids actually go to this school?" I asked.

"Four right now," Mrs. Sanchez said. "We had six last year, but two graduated."

"Doesn't the board hate spending money to make changes just for a few students?"

"Once we adapt something, it's done," Mrs. Sanchez said. "It's good for any new students who need it, or faculty, or visitors even. One of our seniors this year, her father had a stroke. He'll be able to attend her graduation, no problem."

We rode the elevator with two freshman girls who were carrying a giant roll of poster paper. Mrs. Sanchez was right—the elevator was a help to everyone, not only us wheelchair-users.

After a peek into an English lit discussion and a Spanish conversation class, we rode back down to the ground floor. "Let me show you the gym," Mrs. Sanchez said. "We're all really proud of it!"

"Gym?" I repeated. "I won't be taking gym, will I?"

"It's a school requirement," Mrs. Sanchez said with mock indignation. "Two years minimum!"

The gym was partitioned into three sections. In the first, a bunch of boys were shooting baskets. I recognized the boy named Brandon, the one who wanted to try for the varsity team. He was pretty good. I hoped he would make it.

In the next section of the gym, several girls were trying to turn cartwheels as their teacher cheered them on. Music billowed from the third section, where a class in modern dance was underway. As we paused to watch, my heart gave a leap of excitement. There among the dancers, seated in a streamlined silver wheelchair, was Aaron.

"I know him!" I whispered, pointing. "We were at Hamilton Hospital together!"

"He just transferred here this fall," Mrs. Sanchez explained. "Watch him dance."

As we watched, two girls and a boy formed a large triangle. As they bowed and twirled on their feet, Aaron zigzagged deftly between them. His chair was light and quick, and his arms and shoulders mirrored the movements of the standing dancers. Aaron was dancing, too.

"This is so cool!" I breathed. "Could I learn to do it?"

"Sure," Mrs. Sanchez said. "We're starting a program for people in the community—kids, adults, anybody who's interested."

I had automatically assumed I would never dance again. But if Aaron could do it, so could I. Suddenly I remembered how left out I felt as Katrina chattered about her trip to Colorado. But I didn't really know yet what was possible for me. Maybe I'd find a way to explore mountain trails and go horseback riding. I might even make a place for myself at those dreaded parties.

As soon as the music stopped, Aaron raced over to join us. "Amber!" he cried. "Are you going to switch to this school?"

"I'm thinking about it," I told him. "I'm starting to think about it a lot."

"It's great!" he said, beaming. "I never thought I'd say I like school, but I love it here!"

"See how he tries to butter me up!" Mrs. Sanchez laughed. "Talk to him when I'm not around and get the *real* scoop."

"This *is* real," Aaron insisted. He turned back to me. "Remember what I said last summer in group? About how the rest of the world isn't like Hamilton?"

I nodded. I remembered.

"This place has everything—you can go anywhere, reach anything." Aaron stopped, struggling for the right words. "Nobody acts like they're doing you a favor here. It's like—you're just here, with everybody else."

Mom spoke up for the first time. "It's a wonderful atmosphere. I almost wish I could sign up myself."

Aaron reached over and squeezed my hand. "Amber, you've got to come here! We need you in the dance program!"

The rest of the tour went quickly—the computer lab, the learning center, the cafeteria. Mrs. Sanchez brought us back to the office and we all shook hands. "It's been a pleasure to meet you both," she told us. "If you decide to join us, Amber, we'll be very glad to have you."

I thought of Central High, where I encountered barriers everywhere I turned. I thought of Mr. Hartman and the board, with all their talk about safety and expense. How could I stay there, now that I had seen Open Door? "I think I'll be back," I said. "You'll be seeing me again."

14

I didn't tell Katrina and the boys until we finished our next practice session. Legacy was coming along. We had worked up half a dozen songs, and our repertoire was growing. Katrina figured we should go fifty-fifty—half oldies and half contemporary numbers. "That way we'll always surprise them," she said. "Break up the sets." I wasn't sure it was a good idea, but we sounded better and better no matter what we played.

Katrina's brother had bequeathed us a collection of old lead-sheets when he went off to college. As the boys packed up equipment, Katrina and I sorted through the box, hunting for titles we recognized. This was the opportunity I'd been waiting for. I drew a deep breath and said, "Katrina?"

"What?" she asked, adding another song to the reject pile.

"Nothing," I said quickly. "Never mind."

"Have you ever heard of this one? 'Another You,' by The Seekers?"

I shook my head. "Don't we have any more Rolling Stones? Stuff that's familiar."

"I'm looking, I'm looking," Katrina said. "I don't know where half this stuff came from."

I tried again. "Katrina?"

"What?" she said, giving me a sideways glance. "What's the matter?"

I hurled the words out in a rush. "I'm going to leave Central. I'm transferring to Open Door."

The room fell suddenly silent. Pete and Michael stared at me as if I'd just announced that the world was scheduled to end in twenty minutes.

Katrina was the first to speak. "They can't make you!" she cried. "That's not fair!"

"They aren't making me," I insisted. "It's my own choice. I want to go."

"Why?" Pete demanded. "You're doing great at Central."

"You said you'd never go to a school for handicapped people," Katrina reminded me. "Remember? I'm talking last Monday!"

"I know," I said. I was starting to feel confused. I had said those words to Katrina. I had said them to everyone who would hold still!

"They brainwashed you," Pete said gravely. "You know, like in this movie I saw. They put these headphones on you and it whispers in your ear while you're sleeping: 'Open Door! Open Door! I want to go to Open—'"

"It's not just for people with wheelchairs," I said. "It's for everybody. They've got elevators and ramps and everything."

"They haven't got *us*!" Katrina pointed out. "You'll be leaving all your friends!"

"I know," I said. "I didn't want to tell you at first."

Katrina pressed her point harder. "We've been friends since sixth grade! You can't just turn around and leave!"

"How would you like to have people carrying you up and down steps all day?" I demanded. "How would you like to wait for the custodian to show up with the elevator key?"

"I'd hate it!" she agreed. "But I wouldn't leave all my friends just because Heartless is being heartless!"

"How about if they gave you your own elevator key?" Pete asked. "Would you change your mind?"

"There would still be steps to get in and out of the building," I said. "And those heavy doors you've got to push."

"They could build you a ramp," Katrina said. "That wouldn't be hard. Like the one your folks put in."

"They're not going to!" I exclaimed. "At Open Door I can go everywhere and do everything. Why should I stay at Central? You wouldn't if you were me!"

"What if Hartman changed his mind?" Pete asked. "You'd stay then, right?"

"You don't get it," I said in frustration. "My mom's been trying really hard."

Michael was standing by the door to the garage, a little apart from the rest of us. Now he spoke for the first time. "Still," he said. "What if?"

It was one of his typical half sentences, but it thudded down among us with all the weight of truth.

Because classes were well underway, Mrs. Sanchez suggested I finish out the quarter at Central. I had another four weeks to complete papers and group projects, to close out the academic part of my life at school. Most important

to me, I had four weeks in which to say good-
bye to my friends, to let go of my old life once
and for all.

Sometimes I agonized that I had chosen the
easy way out. After all, Open Door wasn't the
real world, the world where I would live for the
rest of my life. But why should I stay at Central
and waste my energy on needless struggle? At
Open Door I could focus on my classes, join
clubs, and try to find new friends. I wasn't
retreating to Open Door, I was moving forward.
This was a healthy, positive decision. I was
transferring to a school where I would be welcome, where I would have every chance to
participate fully.

Yet hard as I tried to embrace the change, I
knew that Katrina was right. Open Door had
ramps and elevators and electric-eye doors, but
it didn't have Katrina, or Cori Madison, or Pete,
or Michael. It didn't have any of the kids whom
I had known for so many years. And it didn't
have Eric Moore.

What did I care about leaving Eric, I asked
myself sternly. *If anything, I should rejoice at the
prospect of getting away from him.* But I remembered him hunched on the window ledge in the
music wing. That picture of him, troubled and

alone, was locked in my mind. Wherever I went it haunted me. What was Eric struggling with? What did he want to say to me? I couldn't leave Central High until I found out.

One night, in my new first-floor room, I stayed up till one writing Eric a note. After two hours I surveyed the crumpled pages scattered over my desk and admitted defeat. I wanted to tell him I was finally ready to talk. I wanted to let him know I would listen to him, no matter what he wanted to tell me. I arranged and rearranged the words, but still they sounded hollow and false. Yes, I could listen to Eric. I could let him unburden his heart. But what could I say to him in return? Perhaps I carried burdens of my own. It was time to lay them aside, to let them go.

The next morning I arrived at school determined to find Eric. His locker and homeroom were on the second floor, so I couldn't look for him there. I had no idea which stairway he would use, so I couldn't sit and wait for him at the bottom. Then I thought of the Learning Center. One long-ago morning Katrina and I had set out to find him there, before Mr. Hartman got in our way. Maybe Eric liked to stop there before the bell. Perhaps I could find him there now.

The Learning Center was one of the nicest

features of Central High. It was a high, airy room filled with sunlight from a wall of windows. Mr. Wong, the librarian, liked to spread books and magazines on the tables, open to stories that always tempted my interest. There were comfortable chairs and a long sofa. There were videos, CDs, and a row of computers. I peered through the doorway, scanning the faces in the room. Eric wasn't at the computers, and I nearly turned away, discouraged. But something prodded me to go inside and get a closer look. Eric sat at a back table, writing in a notebook.

If I stopped to think, I knew I would lose my nerve. I didn't give myself time to plan. I put my hands to the wheels and rolled up beside him. "Hi," I said, taking a deep breath. "I was hoping I'd find you in here."

Eric dropped his pen. He stared at me, speechless.

Now that I'd come this far, I couldn't turn back. "You sent me a letter last summer, remember?"

"Of course I remember," Eric said quietly. "You never answered."

"I know," I said. "That was dumb. I'm sorry." I hadn't expected to say that. Eric was the one who owed the apologies.

"Can we talk now?" Eric asked.

I glanced around to make sure no one sat within earshot. "Okay," I said after a moment. "I think we better."

Eric turned his chair to face me. "There isn't much to say, really," he began. "I was a jerk last spring. I thought I could do anything and get away with it. It was like nothing bad could ever happen to me."

Nothing bad did *happen to you,* I wanted to shout. *It happened to me, to your innocent passenger!* Somehow I choked back the words and let him go on.

"I was into showing off," he said. "Getting people to notice me, you know?"

I nodded. I knew all right!

"I should never have done what I did," he said, and his voice shook. "You got hurt, and it was all my fault."

It was true, what I'd noticed that first day by my locker. Eric's face had changed. He seemed older than he was last spring—not only in months and days but in experience. His old bravado was gone, and in its place I found something gentler, more reflective. I wanted to reach over and take his hand, to assure him that it was all right.

But how could I say that, when he had caused the accident with his wild driving? How could I ever truly forgive him?

My thoughts swept back to the night of Cori's party. I remembered stopping at Lil's Pizza, Eric parking in front of the fire hydrant. I remembered my dash inside for the pie, my rush back to Eric's car. Again I felt the sickening lurch as the car leaped forward to race Eric's friends from the football team. I heard my own voice crying, "Be careful! This road has a lot of tricky curves!" I was hanging onto the pizza box that threatened to slide off my lap, holding it with both hands as though nothing else mattered. That big awkward box kept both my hands busy from the moment I scrambled back into the passenger seat . . .

The room grew unbearably hot. I heard a roaring in my ears, like the ocean far away. "Eric," I said slowly, "it was my fault, too."

"What do you mean?" he demanded. "I'm the one who was speeding!"

"But, Eric," I said, "I didn't fasten my seat belt."

"It isn't the same," he protested. "You'd have been fine if I drove right."

"But if I'd had my seat belt on, I wouldn't

have fallen out when the door popped open. I wouldn't have broken my back."

For a while after that neither of us could find anything to say. We just sat there in the Learning Center, looking at each other and trying to absorb the truth. Something deep within me was easing, uncoiling, letting go. I wasn't angry at Eric any more. Strangely, I wasn't even angry at myself. I had relived that momentous night so many times in the hospital, reworking it again and again in my imagination so that I walked away on two feet. But I had never reached the point where I clicked my seat belt together. I had never let myself look at my own share.

I was sure to be looking at it now. But no amount of fantasy, no amount of regret could undo what had happened. I couldn't spend my life crying over the past. I still had a future ahead of me.

"I'm not mad or anything," I told Eric. "It feels better when I'm not wound up in blaming anybody."

"It feels better just talking," he said. "I had to tell you how sorry I am."

"It's okay," I said. "It really is going to be okay."

This time I did take his hand. We sat there

together in the Learning Center, computers beeping in the background, and the warmth of his hand flowed all through me. Even when the bell rang, we didn't move for a long time. Neither one of us wanted to break the spell.

15

~~~

After Legacy practice the next Saturday, Katrina and I went down to the ice cream shop on South Main Street. It was our favorite hangout; there were no steps at the door, so I could enter without any trouble. We took a booth and I transferred from my wheelchair to the padded bench. "I can't wait to get one of those neat chairs like Aaron and Mrs. Sanchez have," I told Katrina. "They're lightweight, and they fold up really small. They look totally cool."

"Where can you get one?" she asked, rolling my old clunker out of the way into a corner.

"Some woman builds them out in California. She uses a chair herself, and she got sick of the yucky hospital kind."

"Are you glad about going to Open Door?" Katrina asked with a worried frown.

"I wouldn't say glad, exactly. But it makes sense. I guess I'm ready."

"If Hartman came around," she asked carefully, "would you change your mind?"

I shook my head. We'd been over this ground before, and I had nothing new to say. I picked up the menu and studied the sundaes.

But Katrina would not be dismissed. "We've been thinking," she said meaningfully. "We have an idea."

"Who's 'we'?"

"Oh, a bunch of us. Did you know Cori's dad works for the *Weekly Record*?"

"What's that got to do with anything?"

"The power of the press," Katrina intoned, as though she were giving a speech. "The media can turn the tide!"

Her words revolved slowly through my mind. "What tide?" I asked inanely.

"The tide that's pushing you out of Central," Katrina said. "If we got a story in the *Record*, the board would have to think some more."

"I don't want to be in the paper again!" I groaned. "I had enough of that last spring!"

"This'll be different," she insisted. "It'll have a purpose to it."

The waitress came for our orders, but as soon as she was gone, Katrina got back to her argument. "The school is being stupid," she said. "We've got to let people know."

"The board is people, and it knows already," I pointed out. "Even Heartless is people."

"That's debatable," Katrina muttered, and we both laughed.

"I'm not a story now," I said. "Not one that's newsworthy."

Katrina was in planning mode. "We can tell everybody about the key to the freight elevator. Talk about stupidity!"

She was so eager, brimming over with good intentions. But to me the whole idea was mortifying. I searched frantically for escape. "You can't make a story out of an elevator key," I said. "Talk about petty!"

"That's the whole point!" she said. "Wait till people find out their tax dollars are paying for that kind of petty attitude!"

"If it got in the paper at all, it'd probably just be some little paragraph on the back page," I tried again. "Nobody'd ever see it."

"My mom says we should do what they did in the sixties," Katrina explained. "We'll make a story. We'll demonstrate."

This was really getting out of hand. "Katrina!" I pleaded. "I don't want people carrying placards about me! I'd be so embarrassed!"

"Oh," she said, looking down at the formica. "I guess I didn't think about that."

"It'd be awful!" I rushed on. "It's bad enough getting hauled up and down the steps! I don't want a picture of it in the paper."

"It's not to make people feel sorry for you," Katrina insisted. "It's to get them to put in a ramp!"

I thought of Mrs. Sanchez. I remembered what she said about Open Door, how she hoped other schools would follow its example. "If they did build one," I said slowly, "it wouldn't just be for me. It'd be there for everyone who needs it, even after I graduate."

"Right!" Katrina said. "We can demonstrate for—what do they call it?—access. Access for everybody."

"For other kids who might come later on," I mused. "Or maybe a teacher. Or somebody's parents."

"Maybe a new principal," Katrina said with a wicked grin. "Wouldn't that be nice?"

The waitress returned and set our sundaes in front of us. For a while our attention was taken up with hot fudge and dripping whipped cream. This time it was my turn to pick up the demonstration topic again.

"When did you get this idea?" I asked. "You

sound as if you've got it all worked out."

"What makes you think it was my idea? I don't get the credit for this one."

"Who does, then?" I asked, startled. "Cori?"

Katrina put down her spoon and looked at me hard. "No," she said. "It was Eric. Didn't you guess?"

I reeled back in my seat. "Eric?" I gasped. "Eric Moore?"

"*The* Eric," Katrina said. "The Eric that doesn't want you to leave Central High."

"He doesn't?" I repeated. "How do you know?"

"Because I can tell, that's all," Katrina said. "He doesn't want you to leave, and neither do I."

"I don't want to leave either," I heard myself saying, with a fierce certainty I didn't know I possessed. "I want to stay at Central with all the people I care about! With you. And Eric, too!"

"Then let us help you," Katrina said. "We want to."

"Okay," I said. "And Katrina—thank you."

Once we determined to hold a demonstration, things moved amazingly fast. Katrina's mother helped a crowd of us girls make signs and sandwich-board placards. As we worked, she enthralled us with stories of marches on the Pentagon during the Vietnam era, and even taught us a couple of chants and songs.

Three days before Protest Friday, Katrina and I started phoning everyone we knew, urging them to call all of their friends in turn. To my amazement, most people already knew what was going on. Eric had organized his own call system, and he was several steps ahead of us.

Telling kids about the demonstration wasn't embarrassing after all. It was actually fun. It was like inviting the whole school to a giant party. Everybody wanted to come. I knew the enthusiasm wasn't only about me. Sure, most people were sympathetic and wanted me to have the run of the whole school building. But they were also thrilled by the secret plans, the tingling sense of conspiracy. We, the students, were scheming to overturn the authorities and change the rules.

All the kids at school knew what was going on, yet everyone was sworn to silence. Advance word must not reach Mr. Hartman or the school board. As Katrina's mom put it, "Surprise is your greatest ally."

The night before the demonstration, I

summoned my courage and called Eric. "Listen," I began, "I don't know how to thank you, but I've got to try. Thank you for getting this all started."

"It's nothing to thank me for," he said. "It's what I want to do."

Why, I wanted to ask him. *Is it because you still feel guilty over the accident? Is this your way of making it up to me?*

Those hard questions swirled through my head, but I couldn't bring them into the open between us. "It really means a lot," I told him. "It matters, that you're with me on this. That the idea for it came from you."

"I'm acting in my own best interest," he said with a laugh to lighten the moment. "I don't want you to leave Central. If a picket will help, let's picket!"

The next morning was clear and sunny. A crisp, cool breeze sent dry leaves frisking along the sidewalks. Mom drove me to school early and followed as I made my way through the milling crowd of kids around the front entrance. Several people already carried signs, and three or four wore the placards we had made in Katrina's basement. "STAIRS ARE RETRO," read one. Another said, "WHEEL POWER! RAMP

IT NOW!" A third placard proclaimed, "CENTRAL HIGH IS FOR EVERYONE. ACCESS RULES!"

"This is terrific!" Mom exclaimed. "I wish I'd thought of it myself!"

"You tried to negotiate," I said. "You tried everything you could."

"Do you want me to put one of these on?" she asked dubiously, picking up a placard.

"No," I assured her. "You probably shouldn't even hang around. We want them to know this was the kids' idea. It's a better story that way."

Mom looked relieved. I knew she supported what we were doing, but this kind of confrontation wasn't her style. "Call me at lunchtime," she said. "I want to hear all about it."

Ryan Gray and Eric worked their way through the crowd, getting kids into a ragged formation. "We're going to march all the way around the building," Eric said. "We'll station a group at each entrance. You offer leaflets to everybody who goes in, okay? Don't block the doors, just hand them these flyers."

"And sing!" Katrina chimed in. "We've got to sing! 'We shall not, we shall not be moved . . .'"

"Give me a break!" Robin Kozlowski

groaned. "I'll feel like the biggest dork!"

"You won't have to sing by yourself," Katrina insisted. "You're part of a group."

"Where's Heartless?" Ryan asked. "He'll probably start lobbing tear gas as soon as he sees us."

"He's not here yet," Eric said. "His car's not in the faculty lot."

"Come on," called Katrina. "Let's start marching! He'll see us when he gets here."

Slowly at first, starting and stopping, breaking and forming again, the line of marchers began to move. It snaked its way along the front of the building and folded around the far corner. I took my place beside Katrina, rolling slowly forward, trying not to run over anyone's heels. I couldn't take my eyes off Eric as he patrolled up and down, cheering us on, giving directions, shepherding the stragglers back into place. He was the same Eric I'd known last spring—strong, compelling, vividly alive. Yet he was different, too. Instead of making jokes to be the center of attention, he spoke with purpose and clarity. Eric was someone to respect. If only I were at his side, I'd never feel sad or isolated again.

But Eric didn't want me in that special way. He wanted to make amends to me—that was why he led the march today. By fighting for me to stay at Central, he hoped he could assuage his guilt over the accident. He hadn't taken in what I told him, that we each had our share of responsibility for what happened. He couldn't understand that I didn't blame him any longer.

We made a full circuit around the building, groups of kids peeling off to stand at each of the six doors. I returned to the front entrance and stationed myself at the foot of the steps. A camera flashed, and I glanced up to see a burly gray-haired man who had to be Cori's father. "Let me get a shot of your sign," he said. "There—that's perfect!"

The sign on the back of my chair declared, "IT DOESN'T MATTER HOW WE CLIMB, AS LONG AS WE ALL GET TO THE TOP."

"Who thought that one up, anyway?" Eric asked, coming up behind me.

"I did," I said. "Katrina and I had a brainstorming session one night."

"I like it," he said, squatting down to be at my level. "It's kind of like, hey, we're all in this together."

Our eyes met, and we both smiled. We were locked on that moment, sweet and long, when someone called, "Here he comes!" and Mr.

Hartman loomed into view. He was shouting as he came, and his face was red with anger.

"What's going on here?" he bellowed. "You kids get inside! This is a high school, not a circus!"

The camera flashed again, catching him in mid-shout. The instant he saw the press, he spluttered into speechless fury.

"One, two, three!" Katrina cried, and she and I began to sing. Our voices rose alone through the first two lines, and then others began to join us. They sang shyly at first, glancing around to be sure no one was mocking them. But soon our voices gained power. As Mr. Hartman stared, outraged and helpless, we sang in unison, "Just like a tree that's standing by the water,/ We will not be moved!"

After the reporters and the camera crew left school, Mr. Hartman summoned me for a talk. Mrs. Gambino met me at the door to the office, clucking sternly as a flustered hen, and led me through the labyrinth to the principal's inner sanctum. "What do you have to say for yourself, young lady?" Mr. Hartman demanded. "If you weren't in a wheelchair, you'd be suspended on the spot for creating a spectacle like that!"

"If you think I deserve to be suspended, don't let my wheelchair stop you," I said. I could hardly believe those bold words had come out of my mouth.

"We've bent over backwards to be kind to you," Mr. Hartman said after a stunned pause. "We've tried to make you comfortable and keep you safe. And you repay us by complaining, and making demands, and bringing in the media, as if you'd been mistreated."

"This building has three levels and I've been restricted to one," I said. "The same thing would happen to any other person who uses a wheelchair. It isn't fair."

"If I suspend you, it will only play into your hands," he said, as though he were thinking out loud. "I'd be tarred and feathered on the news." He glared at me and said coldly, "Go back to class." I was dismissed.

The protest at Central High was big news that weekend. It appeared as the lead story in the *Weekly Record*, and I was interviewed on the local cable TV station. The *Chicago Tribune* picked up the story and gave it two columns on the Suburban Page. The picture featured Eric and me, seated side by side on a bench in front of the school building. The caption read, NOT

EVEN TRAGEDY CAN STOP THIS
COURAGEOUS YOUNG WOMAN FROM
SEEKING TO LIVE A NORMAL LIFE. I didn't
like the word "courageous," and I flinched when
I read the word "tragedy," too. I was still alive
and well. I went to school, I sang in a band, and
I had friends. There was even a hint of romance
creeping into my life. The accident wasn't a
tragedy. It was an event that had changed my
life in some major ways. But in the most important ways of all, my life was very much the same.

Even with all the uproar, I didn't hold out
much hope. We had made Mr. Hartman so
angry he'd never change his mind now. He'd be
only too delighted to get rid of me. "Backlash,"
Katrina's mother called it. Backlash was always a
possibility.

On Sunday afternoon, Mrs. Sharpless from
the school board called and spoke to Mom for a
long time. "They're having a special teleconfer-
ence tonight," Mom told me when she hung up.
"Bonnie Sharpless says they're 'going to recon-
sider what accommodations can be made.'"

"I'm not getting my hopes up," I said. "At
least I know we tried. You and me and all the
kids at school. Everybody pitched in for me. I
can't ask for more than that."

16

~~~

Despite all the excitement over Protest Friday, Monday morning felt like business as usual. One of the Key Club guys was supposed to meet me at the side entrance at eight o'clock, but he wasn't there when I arrived. I moved out of the line of traffic and waited as kids drifted past me and into the building. Two girls from Chorale stopped to say they loved my picture in the *Tribune*. A boy I'd never seen before—chunky, with a shy smile—said his mother had sent a letter to the school board on my behalf.

"That's so nice of her!" I told him fervently. "Thank her from me, okay?"

Finally a couple of sophomore boys offered to pull me in my chair up the steps. "We saw you on TV," one of them exclaimed. "You're a celebrity!" Would they have offered, I wondered, if they hadn't seen me on cable news? If I went to Open Door, I wouldn't have to wait for help in the mornings. I wouldn't have to ask myself why people volunteered and whether they would feel burdened if I needed their help again.

Inside, I maneuvered to my locker through the crowded corridors. Katrina had left me a note, explaining that she had to get extra help with math before the bell. *Yes*, I thought, *it was an ordinary day again*. What had we accomplished with our placards and our singing? The school board would never budge. Why should Central High accommodate me, when I could be sent safely away?

I still felt out of place in homeroom, down here with the Gs instead of with the Ns upstairs where I belonged. This morning Mrs. Bloomfield was handing out appointment slips for each of us to talk to the guidance counselor about college plans. She called our names alphabetically, from Lindsay Gaddis to Will Gutnik. I came last, a glaring misfit, "Amber Novak."

I started to wheel up to her desk, but she hurried forward and handed me two folded sheets of paper. One was the guidance appointment. The other was a note from Mrs. Gambino. "Mr. Hartman requests to see you during first period," it read. "Please be prompt."

The message had such a cold, commanding tone, I knew it did not bode well. I sat for a few minutes in a daze, too stunned to think. At last I slipped from the room, two minutes before the bell, and made my way to the office.

Mrs. Gambino, greeted me as usual. "Go on in," she said, waving me forward. "You know the way by now." I had never seen her smile that way before, though. Her lips twitched, her eyes almost twinkled. She was barely suppressing a mischievous grin, as if she knew a secret.

Undoubtedly she did, I thought grimly. Whatever Mr. Hartman had to tell me, Mrs. Gambino had an advance preview. Maybe that quirky grin meant that they had won. My friends and I had staged Protest Friday, but we were beaten, nonetheless.

Mr. Hartman sat in his swivel chair behind his desk. "Good morning, young lady," he said. "I suppose you've heard about the board meeting last night."

"Sure," I said. "Mrs. Sharpless called my mom."

"Then you know all about it," he said,

sounding relieved. "I can't to go into details right now, there are still things to be worked out."

"Wait," I said. "I know they had the meeting. I don't know what they decided!"

"They decided," he began, and corrected himself hastily, "*we* decided that I should give you this."

Without rising he rolled his chair around the end of the desk. I'd never realized that his fancy swivel chair was a wheelchair in disguise. It was the sort of wheelchair people aspired to, I thought—a sign of power and prestige.

I was so busy thinking about Mr. Hartman's chair that at first I didn't notice the object he held, small and silvery, dangling from a leather thong. For a long moment I gazed at it, uncomprehending. Then I reached out my hand and took it reverently. "It's the key," I said in awe. "The elevator key! For me!"

Mr. Hartman launched into a meandering lecture about the virtues of flexibility. He explained that Central High could indeed be flexible, within reason. Special exceptions could be made under exceptional circumstances. The freight elevator was a case in point. I must be responsible about its use. The privilege was not extended to everyone.

I listened in a daze, trying to absorb what the

growing heap of words meant for my life. The board had come around. I could use the elevator freely. Ramps would be built, and another "handicapped stall" would be added in the second-floor girls' bathroom. I could stay at Central High. It was a cautious welcome, and it would not have come without our protest. But I could stay here with my friends. I wouldn't transfer to Open Door after all.

On my way out of the office, I called a jaunty good-bye to Mrs. Gambino. This time her grin was unmistakable. "Looks like we'll be seeing you around for a while," she said.

"I guess so," I answered, beaming. "Till graduation!" Joyfully, triumphantly, I swung the key up and down. It spun and danced on its leather thong, so small and yet so powerful!

I was supposed to go straight to Algebra Two, my first-period class, which was well underway. But I wasn't ready to think about quadratic equations. I sped through the empty corridor to the freight elevator. How many times had I waited here for a custodian to work his magic? Now that power rested in my own hands. Stretching up as high as I could, I reached the keyhole beside the door. I turned the key, waited for the green light, and pressed the button marked UP. From the depths of the basement came a groan of cables.

Then the steel doors rumbled apart, and the car waited, inviting me inside. I rolled in and pressed the "2" button. Alone and unassisted, I rose swiftly to the second floor.

From end to end of the long main corridor I rode, zooming past the science labs, the foreign language wing, the office of the school newspaper. Like a time-traveler, I explored places I hadn't seen since last spring. Retracing a long-familiar path, I glided around the bend past the Key Club headquarters and rolled to a stop in front of Eric's locker. From my backpack I took a notepad and pen. "Dear Eric," I began. I paused and took a long look at the word "dear" before I went on. "I am hand-delivering this note. Right this moment, I'm sitting by your locker, wishing you were here—"

"Amber!" came a voice behind me. "Amber, I never thought I'd see you up here!"

Eric strode toward me, his face shining. "I forgot my lit book," he said. "I had to come up and get it."

"I had to come up here, too," I said. "As soon as I got the key. I wanted to tell you before anyone else."

"You got the key!" he repeated. "They finally gave it to you!"

"It's all settled," I said. I held up the key to prove it.

"What about the rest? Like the steps to the entrance." Eric's tone was guarded, as though he didn't dare hope.

"They're going to put in two ramps," I said. "One at the side entrance, and one around back by the gym."

"Not as good as Open Door," Eric said. He studied my face, searching for my response.

"It won't be Open Door," I agreed. "But maybe it's on its way."

"You're staying then?"

"Sure, I'm staying! That's what the protest was about, remember?"

Eric crouched beside me and took both my hands in his. "I was so afraid it wouldn't work," he sighed. "I thought, what if we did the whole demonstration and nobody listened? I wanted to do something, but I knew it still might not be enough."

"You didn't have to do it, you know," I said. "I mean, you don't need to to make anything up to me."

"It wasn't like that," Eric said. "Not like you think."

"I don't blame you for the accident anymore,"

I told him. "I used to, but I don't now."

"You do one stupid thing, and it changes your whole life, and other people's lives, too," Eric said. "I'll always wish that night never happened."

"But my life is okay," I said. "It really is. You need to know that, deep down."

I thought I saw a glint of tears in Eric's eyes. He looked away. "I guess I'm starting to get it," he said. He paused before he looked back at me. "And I'm starting to see what a totally neat girl you are."

"Me?" I asked, with a catch in my throat.

"I thought, if you left Central, how would I get to know you? I'd end up losing you completely. I couldn't stand it!"

"It's taken me a long time to see who you are, too," I said slowly. "I didn't even want to speak to you at first. And now—"

"And now here we are."

"Yes," I said. "Here we are. It feels like this is a beginning."

"It is," he said. "If you want it to be."

It might have felt awkward, leaning from my wheelchair for our first kiss. But we were drawn to each other so powerfully there was no question about logistics. Our lips met, soft and sweet.

The second-floor hall disappeared, and the whole world became nothing but him and me.

"People are going to say a lot of weird things about us," Eric said when we drew apart at last. "Like they might think I'm with you because I feel guilty."

"Or sorry for me," I said. "Do you, sometimes?"

"I feel like you're the girl I want to be with most," he said. "Whenever I go through all this stuff in my mind, I come back to that."

"It'll take a long time to know for sure," I told him. "Anything between us is going to be complicated."

"Is it for you?" he asked.

I thought hard. I tried to look deep within myself, to search out the truth. "No," I said. "It'll seem complicated to other people, I think. But it isn't for me."

The bell rang. Up and down the hall doors burst open, and a human tide swept out to engulf us. Eric walked me to the elevator, the two of us parting the crowd as we made our slow way forward. I didn't care if we ever got there at all. On the outside, I was one more student trying to reach my next class. But on the inside, I was singing.

17

~~~

It was almost Christmas when Legacy gave its first public performance. I arranged the gig myself. We weren't getting paid, I admitted when I told the others, but we'd get exposure and experience. And it would be exposure in the big city! How many other bands could boast as much?

So, on a Saturday morning in mid December, we piled into Pete's parents' minivan and drove to Hamilton Hospital on the Chicago lakefront. I'd been back to Old Alice a couple of times for follow-up appointments, but today was different. This time I wasn't here as a patient. I was the entertainment for a party on D-4.

The past reached out to surround me as we got off the elevator. I knew the clatter of carts, the smell of medicines and antiseptics, even the bright-colored posters on the walls. I had spent four months on D-4. Much of the time I'd been sad, resentful, and downright angry. But I'd had wonderful times, too, with Aaron and Amy and my other friends. I delighted in coming back. I cruised up and down the corridor, searching for familiar faces, smiling at everyone.

"Hey, there, Amber Novak! How's life on the outside?"

I'd know that big, comfortable voice anywhere. Hazel, the nurse formerly known as the Midget, hurried toward me with outstretched arms. She knelt down and gave me a hug.

"Outside is pretty good, actually," I said. "It's good to be back, too."

"For a visit, anyway," she said, completing my thought. "It's a nice place to visit, but you wouldn't want to live here."

"Speaking of living," I said, "we're buying a new house."

"Oh?" Hazel asked. "You're moving away?"

"It's just two blocks from where we are now," I explained. "It's all on one floor, that's the main thing. My dad says as long as I'm using a wheelchair, we ought to have a house I can really live in."

"Good thinking," Hazel said. "It sounds great."

"I better get down to the lounge," I said. "We're setting up. You're coming to our concert, right?"

"Wouldn't miss it!" she exclaimed. "I've got to be able to say, 'I knew her when!'"

Down in the lounge Katrina and the boys had already set up our amps and speakers. We weren't using much equipment, since the space was so small. Kids from the ward crowded around to watch. Most of the faces were new, but I recognized Melissa. She'd had some more problems, she told me, though she didn't want to go into details. They'd put her back in the hospital just when she thought all her health trouble was behind her. She sounded very discouraged, but she perked up when Pete started setting up the drums. By 2:30, when we finally began, every seat in the room was filled. People stood in the doorway and even out in the hall. Several of the nurses looked in, and even Carlos slipped inside to listen. We played a variety of numbers—loud and mellow, fast and slow. Between songs I spoke to the audience. "How's the food in here these days?" I asked. "Do they still serve up those melted vegetables? You know, the ones they boil so long they all kind of squish together?"

Everybody groaned appreciatively, and I went on. "I complained about everything when I was in here last summer. The food, my rehab program, everything. I never thought I'd come back here by choice!"

"You nailed that one!" said a dark-haired girl near the window. She sat in one of those battered hospital wheelchairs, the kind with tape on the frayed armrests.

"But now that I'm here," I went on, "I'm remembering how everybody was really pretty cool. I learned a lot here. They helped me when I needed help. And sometimes, when I needed to do things for myself, they were really mean and they wouldn't help me at all!"

I glanced over at Carlos. Our eyes met, and he grinned.

"Cut the pep talk!" Pete exclaimed. "We're here to play music!" And we launched into our next number.

As the last song on the program, we played that old standard by the Beatles, "Yesterday." Strengthened by the microphone, my voice swelled into the room. I felt the sadness of the lyrics, the mourning for a day that would never come again, a yesterday when all my troubles seemed so far away.

Yet, as I sang those sorrowful words, they no longer pierced me to my heart. "Yesterday" didn't apply to me anymore. My troubles were far away today, as I made my singing debut with Legacy. Katrina, Pete, and Michael were here beside me. Tonight, Eric and I were going to a play at school. I had signed up for the wheel-chair dance class at Open Door. Maybe I'd dance at the prom after all.

While the others hauled equipment, I made my way among the kids in the lounge, trying to greet as many as I could. When I reached the girl by the window, she said her name was Hannah and she'd been at Hamilton for a month. "I had meningitis," she explained. "Now they say I'm not going to be able to walk again." She spoke flatly, as if the words had no real meaning for her.

"I couldn't believe it when they told me, either," I said. "Now I believe it when I'm awake, but in my dreams I still walk around on my feet."

"Do you really sing in public?" Hannah asked. "I mean, not just places like this?"

"We're supposed to play at a Sweet Sixteen

party next month," I said. "We even get money for it. That makes us professionals."

Hannah had a great smile. Her eyes danced. "I like to sing, too," she said. "I've got a friend who plays keyboard."

"Amber, come on!" called Katrina. "Can you roll up these power cords?"

"Sure," I said. "Coming."

Hannah followed as I set to work. I sorted out the tangle of wires and wound each one into a neat little pckage. Then it was time for us to go.

"Next time I see you, you'll be winning a Grammy," said Hazel.

"I'll take you out on my yacht," I promised. "Bring the whole ward, and we'll have a party."

"Amber!" Katrina called. "I'm holding the elevator! Come *on!*"

"I guess I've got to go," I said, and rolled down the hall toward the open door.

About the Author

Deborah Kent grew up in Little Falls, New Jersey, where she was the first totally blind student to attend the local public school. She received her B.A. in English from Oberlin College, and earned a master's degree from Smith College School for Social Work. She worked for four years in community mental health at the University Settlement House on New York's Lower East Side.

In 1975 Ms. Kent decided to pursue her life-long dream of becoming a writer. She moved to the town of San Miguel de Allende, Mexico, which had an active colony of writers and artists. In San Miguel she wrote her first young-adult novel, *Belonging*. She also met her future husband, children's author R. Conrad (Dick) Stein. Deborah Kent has published more than a dozen novels for young adults, as well as numerous titles for middle-grade readers. She lives in Chicago with her husband and their daughter, Janna.

It wasn't a dream . . .

TIMELESS LOVE

by Judith O'Brien

It was a lovely silver necklace with a strange antique charm—an early sixteenth birthday present from her parents. But now Samantha clutched the charm, desperate to disappear when her father discovered she'd wrecked his BMW—and suddenly she was standing in the bedchamber of Edward VI, the young king of England in 1553 . . . .

He was her own age—and cute. She should have recognized the danger when the scheming Duke of Northumberland tried to come between them. But Edward protected her, and rumors of marriage began. Sam thought she was safe--until a handsome young stranger stole her heart and swept her into the middle of deadly sixteenth-century court intrigue—could she ever go home again?

Jamie has a secret. . . .

THE NIGHT I DISAPPEARED

by Julie Reece Deaver

Something scary is happening to seven-teen-year-old Jamie Tessman. Ever since she and her mother arrived in Chicago, she's been plagued by freaky mind-slips and vivid daydreams about her sort-of-boyfriend Webb. When Jamie's inner world starts taking her hostage and keeping her imprisoned for longer periods of time, she becomes terrified that she is slowly losing her mind.

Jamie's mom doesn't seem to notice any-thing is wrong. No one does—until Jamie meets Morgan, a new friend who's had her own "brush with nuttiness." When Jamie disappears into her inner world one night and can't find her way out, Morgan sees to it that Jamie finally gets help. Morgan's aunt, a psychiatrist, breaks through Jamie's paralyzing fear and helps her unravel a tan-gle of long-forgotten, horrifying secrets in her past. . . .

**IT WAS A BRILLIANT SCIENTIFIC BREAKTHROUGH.
A GENE THAT MUTATES THE MIND,
THAT GIVES A HUMAN BRAIN ACCESS
TO ALL COMPUTER SYSTEMS.**

**IT IS A DEADLY CURSE. IT CREATES PEOPLE
OF INCALCULABLE POWER, WHO MUST BE
DESTROYED BEFORE THEY CAN GROW UP.**

**IT IS A THRILLER THAT BLASTS YOU
INTO A MIND-BLOWING FUTURE....**

HEX

SHE IS ALL-POWERFUL.
SHE MUST BE DESTROYED!

HEX: SHADOWS

SHE SHOULD BE DEAD.
BUT COMPUTERS ARE HARD TO KILL ...

(COMING IN FEBRUARY 2002)

HEX: GHOSTS

THE GOVERNMENT WANTED THEM DEAD.
THE WORLD WAS NOT READY FOR THEM.
BUT NOW THEY ARE GOING
TO MAKE PEOPLE LISTEN.

(COMING IN JUNE 2002)